EMPTY NET

EMPTY NET

DAVID STARR

James Lorimer & Company Ltd., Publishers
Toronto

James Lorimer & Company Ltd., Publishers acknowledges funding support from the Ontario Arts Council (OAC), an agency of the Government of Ontario. We acknowledge the support of the Canada Council for the Arts, which last year invested $153 million to bring the arts to Canadians throughout the country. This project has been made possible in part by the Government of Canada and with the support of Ontario Creates.

Cover design: Gwen North
Cover image: Shutterstock

978-1-4594-1362-7
eBook also available 978-1-4594-1361-0

Cataloguing data available from Library and Archives Canada.

Published by:
James Lorimer &
Company Ltd., Publishers
117 Peter Street, Suite 304
Toronto, ON, Canada
M5V 0M3
www.lorimer.ca

Distributed in the US by:
Lerner Publisher Services
1251 Washington Ave. N.
Minneapolis, MN, USA
55401
www.lernerbooks.com

Printed and bound in Canada.
Manufactured by Friesens Corporation in Altona, Manitoba, Canada in August 2019.
Job #257897

For Humboldt

Contents

1 THE BURNABY WILDCATS

Focus.

Maddie Snow squared up to face the left wing as she streaked toward her. *What are you going to do?* Maddie asked in her head. *Drive to the net yourself? Or pass off to the centre coming in behind you?*

Maddie flexed her catching hand and squeezed her stick. *You're passing.* She was certain. She almost always was.

The winger crossed the blue line, faked a slapshot. Then, sure enough, she dropped the puck off for the centre. The centre shot a quick snap that lifted the puck off the ice and sent it flying toward the goal.

Maddie was ready. From the second the puck left the stick she saw nothing but the black disc. It was a great shot, fast and high to the glove side. Maddie raised her glove hand and easily caught it.

"Great save, Maddie!" her coach yelled from the bench. Maddie smiled as she flipped the puck to the ref. She could see her mom and dad cheering in the stands, but she quickly turned her attention back to the game.

There would be time for that later. Now she had a job to do.

At almost the end of the third period. Maddie's team, the Burnaby Wildcats, was up 1–0 over the Kelowna Fire. The game had been a close, hard-fought battle. The winner of this game would move on to face the Victoria Blades in the Bantam Provincial Championship in Victoria. The Blades were the best Bantam girls' hockey team in the province. Maddie wanted a chance to play them. She wanted to show them what she and the rest of the Wildcats were made of.

The teams lined up to take the face-off in the Wildcat end. Maddie homed in on the two centres bent over the circle. Maddie read skaters on the ice like a chess player would read a board. She could see plays and passes, figure out moves and counter moves. No matter who won the face-off, no matter where the puck went, Maddie would be ready.

Only forty-five seconds to go. A Kelowna defender picked up the puck and skated hard. Now forty seconds. The Kelowna goalie skated to the bench, giving way for a sixth attacker. It was now or never for the Fire.

Focus.

From inside her crease, Maddie watched as six Kelowna Fire skaters moved toward her. Like a tidal wave, they crossed the centre line, moving toward the Wildcat zone.

Maddie heard nothing but her own breathing and

saw nothing but the skater crossing over the line. *A quick pass to the centre, who will dish it behind her to a defender. That's what they'll do.*

With twenty seconds to go, the Kelowna centre did just that. The defender fired through a forest of legs and sticks toward Maddie. Two teams scrambled like crazy trying to find the puck. But it was Maddie who saw the puck first. It was sitting just inside her crease.

She leapt forward and covered the puck with her glove. The Kelowna players slashed and hacked at her. The whistle blew with fifteen seconds to go. Maddie took her time getting up. Her arm was sore from sticks whacking at her. She'd be bruised black and blue the next day. But right now, Maddie didn't feel a thing.

There were ten seconds to go. The Kelowna defenders tried to fire the puck back toward the forwards crowded around Maddie's net. But Sophia, the Wildcat left wing, broke up the pass with the blade of her stick.

With five seconds to go, there was no time left for Kelowna. The crowd came alive as Ana Lucia rushed to the puck and shot it toward the empty Kelowna net.

The clock counted down three seconds, then two. Just as the clock hit one, Maddie watched the puck cross the goal line at the other end of the rink. The horn sounded, the game ended and Maddie skated out of her net. The Wildcats had done it! They had beaten Kelowna 2–0. Two days from now they would play for the provincial title.

2 THE WORST DAY EVER

"Maddie, can you come to the living room?" Maddie's dad asked. "Mom and I need to talk to you."

"What's up?" Maddie asked. She took a seat next to her parents in the living room. It was a warm March afternoon, three days before the provincial championship and Maddie was feeling good.

"I passed the sergeant's test. I got a promotion," her dad said.

"That's awesome!" Maddie replied. Her dad was a corporal in the Burnaby RCMP. She knew he'd been studying for weeks. "So you're a sergeant now?"

"Yes. Starting September first I am a sergeant."

"That's cool, Dad. I'm proud of you." But Maddie noticed her dad give her mom a strange look.

"There's more," her dad said. "I've been transferred."

"That's no big deal," said Maddie. "You've been transferred before." Maddie's dad had changed detachments a couple of times over the years. Maddie had lived in their Burnaby townhouse her whole life. But before working in Burnaby, he had been stationed in nearby North Vancouver and Coquitlam.

"To where? Surrey? Maple Ridge?" There were lots of areas in Metro Vancouver served by the Mounties.

"That's what I wanted to talk to you about," her dad said. "I've been asked to be in charge of a detachment."

As her dad talked, a weird feeling began growing in Maddie. There was something going on, something strange.

"A place called Fort St. James," her dad said.

"Where's that?" Maddie asked. "By Langley?" Langley was a bit of a drive, especially at rush hour, but nothing her dad couldn't manage.

"No, Maddie." This time it was her mom who spoke. "Fort St. James is one thousand kilometres north. It is up near Prince George in the middle of the province. We are going to have to move. A real estate agent is coming by the house today."

"Move? Sell the house?" Maddie felt as if she had taken a puck to the stomach.

"It's not going to be easy, I know," her dad said. "But it is a great chance for me in my career."

Maddie didn't really hear him. *Move.* The only word Maddie heard was *move.*

"But I don't want to leave my friends," she said. Then a more terrible thought hit Maddie. "What about hockey? We can't leave Burnaby! The Wildcats need me! I'm the starting goalie and the provincial championship is next week! You could say no, right? Tell them you don't want to go?"

"I'm really sorry, Maddie," her dad said. "You'll get to play one more game with the Wildcats. But we won't be here next season."

"Dad, please!" Maddie begged, trying to control her tears. "You can't move us! My whole life is here!"

"It won't be that bad, Maddie," her mom said. "There's a good hockey program in Fort St. James. And who knows? You may like it."

"Like it?" Maddie nearly screamed the word. She stormed out of the living room to her bedroom. "I'll hate it!" she cried, slamming the door shut. "It's the worst thing that's ever happened to me!"

Alone in her room, Maddie sent message after message to her friends with the terrible news. They were as upset as she was, especially her teammates on the Burnaby Wildcats. Maddie was not just the goalie, she was the captain of the team too. The day had started out so well. Now? It had become the *worst* one ever.

★★★

With five minutes to go in the game against the Victoria Blades, the Wildcats held on to a 4–3 lead. They were winning. But Maddie couldn't take credit for it. She was playing one of the worst games of her life and she knew it.

The Victoria crowd was hostile. Normally Maddie

could tune out noise from the fans, but not today. The cheers and the boos were getting to her. To make things worse, she was having a hard time following the play. She couldn't focus on what was happening. Since learning she was moving to Fort St. James, something had changed. She felt nervous and on edge.

Maddie looked at the clock. Four minutes to go. The play was mostly in the Blades' end, with her team pressing hard for one more goal.

Then disaster struck. Ana Lucia fired a rocket at the net. The puck went over the shoulder of the Blades goalie and hit the crossbar hard. Maddie could hear the puck ringing off the iron at the other end of the ice.

The puck flew off, bouncing off the glass. It landed right near the stick of Blades left-wing number nine, a tall girl with a long, red ponytail sticking out from under her helmet.

It happened so fast that the Wildcats could only watch. Number nine picked up the puck and skated hard down the ice on a breakaway. Maddie squared up in the net, watching number nine get closer.

Number nine crossed the blue line. *You're going to try to fake me out and deke right,* Maddie thought. Number nine raised her stick. *A fake, definitely a fake to the right.* Maddie put her weight on her left foot, ready to slide over.

Then number nine shot. It wasn't fancy, just an old-fashioned wrist shot. It lifted the puck half a metre into the air toward Maddie's left side. The puck went over the blade of her stick and into the back of the net.

The score was tied at 4–4 with three minutes to go! The Victoria crowd roared.

"It's okay, Maddie!" her coach yelled from the bench.

But Maddie didn't feel okay, not one bit.

The teams lined up. The linesman dropped the puck to start the play.

Focus, Maddie almost begged herself. The teams were playing for overtime now, nobody wanting to make a mistake.

With two minutes to go, Wildcats defender Sophia poke-checked the puck away from a Blades forward. The puck jetted down the ice toward Maddie. Players from both teams raced for the puck. Maddie's heart fell in her chest when number nine from the Blades got there first.

There was no breakaway this time. Number nine was quickly surrounded by Wildcats. All she could do was shoot the puck toward the net, a gentle shot that Maddie stopped easily with her stick.

"Maddie!"

Maddie looked up the ice to see Ana Lucia open on the left side. Nobody skated faster than Ana Lucia. One quick pass and she would be away! This was the chance the Wildcats needed to win the game.

Maddie was a good puck handler. She'd made passes like this a thousand times. But instead of sending the puck gliding quickly over the ice she whiffed it. The puck wobbled awkwardly away, moving too slowly toward Ana Lucia.

Out of nowhere, number nine skated in and got the puck.

Thirty seconds to go. Maddie watched in horror as number nine skated toward her.

Twenty-five seconds to go. Maddie readied herself for another snapshot. But this time number nine faked, drawing her out of the goal. There was nothing she could do but watch as number nine tapped the puck into the open net.

3 GOALIE CAMP

Fort St. James.

Even the name of the place sounded small and far away. Maddie opened up Google on her phone and typed. What she read did not make her feel better.

The town was very far away. It was small, northern and remote. No mall, no pool and no fast food except for a pizza place. The town was old, Maddie read, not that she cared much about history. First Nations people had lived there for thousands of years. The town started as a fur trading fort two hundred years ago. Now its economy was based on forestry, tourism and mining, things Maddie cared even less about than history.

She kept looking. There was hockey to be sure, like her mom said. They'd even had a few players make the NHL. But the girls' team only went up to Peewee.

A month ago, Maddie had been in a great mood, her summer full of hockey and friends. Now? Her entire life had fallen apart. She was moving from the only home she'd known. She had lost the provincial final for her team and would never play for the Wildcats again. Fort St. James? She may as well be moving to the moon.

Maddie didn't talk to her parents for three days after the loss in Victoria. When they got back home she stayed out of the house with her friends as long as she could. She locked herself in her bedroom when she was home.

Things got worse when the real estate agent put up the "for sale" sign outside their three-bedroom townhouse on Patterson Street. When the "sold" sign went up she cried. It was one thing to know your house was for sale, but something much worse when it actually sold. It meant it was no longer yours. That the move was real.

★★★

"I'm glad we're talking again, Maddie," said her dad. He was dropping her off at 8 Rinks early Monday morning for the first day of summer goalie camp. "How are you doing? You've barely spoken to me since Victoria."

"Pick me up at two, please."

"See you at two, then," sighed her dad.

The only thing that made Maddie forget how terrible her life had become was being on the ice. Thank goodness there was the goalie camp, five days of training. During the morning, the goalies would work on their fitness. They would run, lift weights and work on their stretches. After fitness training, they would lace up the skates. Maddie would work on her angles, on glove, stick and skate saves. She would improve other skills like passing the puck to the defence and poke-checking. The afternoons were for three-on-three games. The coaches had organized members of the Vancouver Giants to play offence and defence, with the camp goalies taking turns in the nets.

The changing room was full of goalies Maddie knew. April was the backup goalie for the Wildcats, Lisa and Nikki were from Coquitlam, and there were goalies from Vancouver, West Vancouver, Delta and other Metro Vancouver cities.

Maddie laid her equipment on the floor in the order she would put it on. Undergarments, pelvic protector, pants and skates came first. Then her goalie pads. She kneeled and strapped them on, starting at the bottom, working her way up to the Velcro straps.

Next came the neck guard, the shoulder and arm pads. Then Maddie put on her Wildcats jersey, the familiar number one sliding into place on her back. She'd worn that number, Roberto Luongo's number, for years. Even though Luongo was no longer a Canuck, he was still her favourite player.

The girls were full of energy as they got into their gear.

"I'm sorry you're not going to be here for the season," April said to Maddie. "I wanted to be the starter.

But not like this."

Ana Lucia and Maddie had battled for starting goalie position for what seemed like forever. Maddie usually won out. But they were friends both on and off the ice.

"Where are you moving to?" asked Karley, a goalie from Pitt Meadows.

"Fort St. James."

"Where's that? I've never heard of it."

Maddie slid her helmet over her face and picked up her stick. "That's because it's in the middle of nowhere."

Maddie left the changing room. She walked across the rubber matting through the tunnel to the players' bench. Then she stepped onto the ice.

All goalies have superstitions. Maddie was no different. She always liked to be the first person on the ice. Maybe it was the sound her skates made as she glided across the freshly washed ice. Maybe it was the sight of her breath rising in a white cloud through her mask. Whatever it was, Maddie always felt better when she came out before anyone else. It helped her focus.

She also had the habit of tapping the goalposts with her stick. Left post first, then right, then left again. Always three taps, always left right left. Maybe she'd seen an NHL goalie do it. Maybe it had been her own idea. All Maddie knew was that tapping the posts three times settled her down and got her ready for the game.

Maddie skated slowly across the ice. Behind her she heard the other goalies chatting as they stepped on the ice. Soon, two dozen goalies, boys and girls from ages twelve to eighteen, were each doing their own ritual.

Everyone loosened up. It had been a while since Maddie had stretched in her full gear, since the terrible loss to Victoria, and it felt good as she worked the kinks out of her legs. Then she heard a whistle.

"Okay everyone, gather round." The instructors had come out of their dressing room. There were four of them, each a former goalie in the NHL or AHL. Two were also goalie coaches with pro teams.

"Let's see how slow you've gotten this summer," said the lead instructor. He dumped a bucket of pucks on the ice and looked at his clipboard. "Madeline Snow."

Maddie was glad to go first. She told herself that it would keep her from thinking about the upcoming move.

Maddie skated to the net. She tapped her posts. Left, right, then left again. "Ready when you are," she said.

The first shot was a wrister a few inches off the ground. Maddie saw nothing but the puck as it left the stick, heard nothing but the sound of the shot.

Focus.

That was Maddie's advantage, the Wildcats' coach had told her. She could focus. The whole world went away when she was in net, her mind and body involved in nothing but the play. Maddie watched the puck come to her like it was in slow motion. She moved her stick a few centimetres, easily making the save with the blade. She breathed a sigh of relief. She'd lost her focus in the provincial final. She was glad to see she still had it.

"Not bad," the instructor said. "Remember, everyone, the difference between a good goalie and a great goalie isn't physical toughness. It is mental toughness. There is no other position that plays with your head as much as playing goal. Be mindful of that. You need to have 100 per cent of your head in the game."

He turned to Maddie. "You ready for something a little harder?"

"Bring it on," Maddie said, getting into her stance.

The coach did. It was a wrist shot again, but this time much faster. The puck flew toward her on her glove side. The puck was speeding through the air, heading to the top corner. But Maddie had it all the way. She flashed out her glove, her timing perfect.

"Not bad," Maddie told the instructor with a grin. "But do you think *you* could try something harder?"

For the next twenty minutes, all the goalies warmed up. "Okay, everyone," the instructor said. "We're going to work you harder than you've ever worked before. Get ready for it. This is going to be the toughest day of your lives!"

Suddenly all the joy Maddie felt being on the ice went away. She thought about the move, of leaving her house, her friends, her school and her team behind forever. *Toughest day of your life?*

The coach had no idea. Losing the provincials was much tougher than goalie camp. But nothing in comparison to losing her team and her friends. The toughest *week* of her life was coming up in August.

4 THE MOVE

Goalie camp ended and Maddie's last few weeks in Burnaby passed by far too quickly. Instead of enjoying the last month of summer holidays, Maddie had to deal with packing up her things. She cried when she saw her empty room.

Maddie went out with her friends when she could. But the move was always in the back of her mind. The worst thing of all was packing up her hockey gear. She had two large bags for her equipment and another for her sticks. Packing them up meant her time on the Wildcats was over.

The moving truck came on the second Monday in August. Maddie couldn't bear to watch. She stayed in her empty room as the movers put her entire life in the large truck. Maddie didn't come out until the last box and bag was packed. She watched the truck drive away in the early afternoon.

She looked sadly around her bedroom. It was completely bare except for a small suitcase, an air mattress and her sleeping bag.

Maddie's dad was set to leave right after the moving truck. He needed to be in Fort St. James the next evening when the truck arrived. Maddie and her mom would meet him at their new house the day after.

Her dad kissed her mom goodbye. He gave Maddie a hug and a kiss as well, though she barely hugged him back.

"Drive safely," Maddie said.

"You too."

Her dad climbed into the cab of his brand new pickup truck, a large silver Ford F-150 he had bought once the house sold. "Everybody drives a truck up north," he had told Maddie. "That's how you get out into the wilderness." Maddie watched her dad drive away. *Enjoy the wilderness?* She would never enjoy the wilderness. She knew she would not enjoy anything about Fort St. James.

On her last day in Burnaby, Maddie went to Metro Mall with her friends. They had lunch at Chronic Taco, her favourite place to eat in the world. She stayed there as long as she could. But finally, she had to go back to her strange, empty home.

For dinner, her mom ordered a deluxe veggie pizza. Maddie and her mom ate sitting on the kitchen floor. When they were done Maddie excused herself. It was early but Maddie wanted to go to bed for the very last time in the only bedroom she had ever known. She lay on the floor, staring up at the ceiling for what seemed like hours.

I'm going to be up all night, Maddie thought as the sun set outside and the room grew dark. Ten minutes later she shut her eyes. Five minutes after that she was fast asleep. Her last night in Burnaby had begun.

★★★

"Goodbye house," said Maddie. Her mom turned her car onto Patterson Street early Monday morning. Their townhouse was nothing special, but it had been home. Leaving it behind felt like leaving a friend. Their house disappeared behind them as they headed north to the Trans-Canada Highway.

The sun was climbing into the sky, lighting up the North Shore Mountains to the east. Looking west, Maddie could see the carnival rides at Playland and the tops of the high-rises of downtown Vancouver. "How long until we get there?" Maddie asked as her mom merged onto the freeway.

"It's six-thirty in the morning now," her mom said. "Fort St. James is just under a thousand kilometres north. Your dad made the drive in eleven hours. The only stops he made were for gas. I thought we'd get breakfast in Hope, stop for a quick lunch in Williams Lake where your dad slept last night and then drive straight through. We should be there by around seven-thirty this evening."

"Great. Thirteen hours in a car. I can hardly wait."

"Come on, Madeline," her mom said a little sharply. Her mom and dad almost always called her Maddie. Her full name was used only when they were mad at her. "It is what it is. You can either be grumpy the whole way or try to enjoy the adventure. Your dad said the trip was beautiful."

"You enjoy the beauty," Maddie said. She put her headphones on. "I'm going to listen to my music and try to sleep."

But Maddie didn't sleep. Through half-closed eyes she watched the lanes full of cars crawling west into Vancouver.

Half an hour later, they had reached Abbotsford, and twenty minutes after that Chilliwack. The city was long gone, replaced by corn fields and farm houses.

They stopped at the McDonald's in Hope for a quick breakfast. Maddie had played in Hope once in a hockey tournament. Hope was small. *But not as small as Fort. St. James*, Maddie thought. *Not by a long shot.*

After Hope the road followed the Fraser River through the mountains.

"Beautiful isn't it," her mom said.

"I guess," Maddie grunted. The day was very warm already, and Maddie could see waves of heat coming off the rocks. The road in the canyon snaked along beside the river, through several tunnels and up the sides of the mountains.

The Move

An hour or so later, they reached the town of Cache Creek where Maddie's mom stopped for gas. The river was nowhere to be seen. The countryside was flatter, with fields and sagebrush.

"It kinda looks like an old western movie," said Maddie. Maddie had been doing nothing but thinking about how unfair life was, how cruel her parents were to force this move on her. It had only been in the last few minutes that she turned her attention outwards. She realized how strange and different this part of the province was.

"It does, doesn't it?" her mom agreed. "There are rattlesnakes and cactus here as well, if you can believe it."

As they drove on, the country changed again. They saw fields of hay and other crops near the road. But in the distance were large mountains, covered in trees and topped with snow.

They passed through several small towns: Clinton, 100 Mile House, Lac La Hache. Just after noon, they arrived in Williams Lake, the largest town they had seen on the drive so far.

"Gas and lunch," her mom said as they pulled into town.

"No takeout. Please?" Maddie asked. Of course she liked fast food. But it had been all they'd eaten for the last two days.

"Fair enough. I don't feel like a hamburger either."

They found a small restaurant called the Gecko Tree

on Mackenzie Avenue. Maddie ordered Eggs Benny and was pleasantly surprised by how tasty her meal was. "Not bad for a small town," Maddie's mom replied, eating a quesadilla. "Maybe Fort St. James has a place like this too."

"Maybe." Maddie wasn't holding out any hope. Williams Lake was tiny compared to Burnaby. But at least it had a McDonald's and traffic lights. Fort St. James had neither.

In less than an hour they were on the road again. Maddie dozed, waking up only for a few minutes when they reached Quesnel. "What's that smell?" she asked, wrinkling her nose.

"That is a pulp mill," said her mom.

***

They reached the "Welcome to Prince George" sign just after four in the afternoon. Maddie was sick of looking out the window, staring at trees and fences. It was hard to believe she was actually looking forward to getting anywhere, even Fort St. James.

Prince George was the largest town they had seen since leaving home. The downtown even had some buildings that were more than six storeys high. But it was much smaller than Brentwood or Metro or any of the high-rise neighbourhoods in Burnaby.

"Prince George has all the big stores you're used

to back home. There is a university here and a great aquatic centre. Your dad says we'll probably come here at least once a month. We are only two hours away from Fort St. James now."

"Great," Maddie said, but she didn't mean it. In Burnaby, Maddie had a ten minute Skytrain ride to Metro Mall and was only thirty minutes away from downtown Vancouver. She could go anytime she wanted. Now? It would take two hours by road through the wilderness to get to this depressing place.

An hour later they reached a town called Vanderhoof. Like a lot of the places they had passed, it was a just few fast food restaurants and other businesses built along the road.

It was in Vanderhoof that Maddie had a thought. If she hated Fort St. James, she would just go back to Burnaby. She had lots of friends. Any one of them would let her stay. The idea gave her hope.

"Almost there," Mom said as she gassed up the car for the last time on the trip. "Another forty-five minutes and we will be in our new home. Next stop Fort St. James."

5 WELCOME TO THE FORT

It was just past seven in the evening but the sky was still bright. Maddie noticed that the sun was higher than it should have been for the time of day.

"That's because we have travelled so far north," her mom explained. "In the summer the days are very long. But in winter it'll be dark not long after three."

The GPS said they were fifteen minutes from their new home when Maddie saw Stuart Lake, a huge body of water to their left. Along the road and the shoreline Maddie saw houses and a church, but nothing else except for a Petro Canada gas station. "Where are the stores?" Maddie asked. "This can't be it. I researched."

"This is the Nak'azdli First Nation," Mom explained. "Fort St. James is just ahead. That's where the shops and services are."

A few minutes later they saw a "Welcome to Fort St. James" sign on their left, next to a sign that pointed to Fort St. James National Historic Site. Just after that they came to a five way stop. Maddie's mom turned left.

"There's the RCMP detachment that your dad will command," she said proudly. She pointed out a newer-looking building on the right, the Canadian flag flying over it.

The road turned to the right and they entered "downtown." To Maddie it looked to be little more than a couple of strip malls joined together. She saw a pharmacy, a clothes store, a few restaurants, a hardware store and a grocery store called Overwaitea. Apart from a few other buildings, that was it.

They crossed over a small bridge and the lake appeared again to their left. "Cottonwood Beach," said Maddie's mom, reading a wooden sign. An old-fashioned plane stood on display on the beach. "It looks cute. This must be where people come and swim and have picnics."

"Turn left on Lakeshore Drive," the GPS voice said. Mom signalled and followed Lakeshore Drive past an old wooden church and a graveyard. "Turn left on Stones Bay Road." They continued along, past the Forest Service headquarters, past a golf course and toward a large mountain with a huge granite face.

"The destination is on your left," the GPS voice piped up one last time. Maddie's mom turned off the road and onto a gravel driveway. A log house with a green tin roof was nestled between several large fir trees at the end of it.

Maddie saw her dad standing on the porch. "You made good time," called her dad as they parked next to his truck. He hugged Maddie and her mom as they climbed out of the car. "Welcome to the Fort. That's what the locals call Fort St. James. You must be starving. I have dinner almost ready for you. Come on inside and check it out."

Maddie looked around as she walked into her new home. She had seen log houses on TV but had never been inside of one.

The new house was much bigger than their townhouse back in Burnaby. A large picture window in the living room looked out onto the lake. Stuart Lake was still as glass, no wind rippling the surface. Off to the side of the window was the kitchen.

"There's a bathroom to the left," her dad said. "Three bedrooms and a bathroom upstairs. A rec room, two more bedrooms and another bathroom in the basement."

"The house is built on a slope," he went on. "Most of the basement is ground level. There's a door and a small porch down there, and the bedrooms have views of the lake. I had the movers take your stuff to the largest room downstairs, Maddie. I figured that would be the room you wanted. But if you want, you can move upstairs."

"I'm sure it will be fine," Maddie said shortly. She looked out the window to the lake. The sun was starting to dip in the west but it was still bright and warm outside.

The town hadn't been much to look at, and Maddie

was still figuring out when she would take off and go back to Burnaby. But she had to admit that the house was very nice, especially with the view.

They'd gone skiing at Whistler once and the place reminded Maddie a bit of the chalet her dad had rented. It was almost like camping in the woods.

"The place came with a great barbeque." Her dad's voice broke into Maddie's thoughts. "I bought some steaks this afternoon. They are on the grill and should be ready soon."

While her dad finished cooking, Maddie walked downstairs. The basement rec room had a cozy feel to it. Her dad had put their old couch and living room chairs down there, along with a large TV.

When Maddie got to the biggest bedroom, she thought her dad had chosen well. Even without seeing the other rooms in the house, Maddie knew this room was the one she would have picked for herself. It was almost twice as big as the one she had back in Burnaby, with a large closet and a view of the lake through her window. The movers had set up everything. All that was left for her to do was to put away her personal things.

"Dinner's ready!" she heard her dad call. Maddie didn't realize how hungry she was until she walked upstairs and smelled the steak.

"I thought we'd eat outside," her dad said. A large deck led off the house from the kitchen. Their patio set was out here, next to the barbeque. Bowls of salad and a plate of baked potatoes were on the table, as well as a pitcher of lemonade.

"Well done, dear," said her mom. "I'm going to expect this sort of meal every day."

It was then that Maddie realized what was missing from her room. "Dad, where's my hockey gear?"

Her dad smiled. "I was wondering when you were going to ask that. Don't worry, it's safe. I'll show you after dinner."

Once they had eaten, Maddie and her dad walked to the side of the house. There were two outbuildings that Maddie hadn't noticed when she arrived.

"The large building is the garage," said her dad. "Heat and power inside, both things we'll need this winter unless we want to spend half an hour scraping windshields."

"And the smaller one?" Maddie asked.

"It's for you." Maddie's dad opened the door of a small, well-built shed. Maddie breathed a sigh of relief when she saw her hockey bags.

"The previous owner's son played hockey too," her dad explained. "I guess his dad didn't want stinky gear inside his house or garage, so he built this place. Power and heat, drying racks and shelves. What do you think?"

"It's okay," Maddie said, though she had to admit it was pretty cool.

Maddie surprised herself with a big yawn. It was only a little past nine, but she had been up for more than sixteen hours.

"Time for you to go to bed," her dad said. "I've got a busy day planned for you tomorrow."

Maddie didn't argue. She said good night to her parents and walked downstairs. It was the strangest feeling to be going to bed in a new room in a new house, a thousand kilometres away from her home.

Though Maddie was tired, she couldn't get to sleep. The light didn't help. It wasn't until well past ten that it started to get dark outside, which Maddie found very strange.

There was something else weird as well. In Burnaby there was always noise. Firetrucks in the distance, the honking of horns, the sound of traffic, even the whine of the Skytrain passing by.

Here there was nothing. A few times Maddie heard the cry of a bird, a haunting sound that echoed across the lake. But that was it. Alone in the quiet of her new room, as tired as she was, Maddie didn't fall asleep for a very long time.

6 MADDIE JOINS THE STARS

"I've already registered you for school," Maddie's dad said as they drove past Fort St. James Secondary School. Her dad was wearing his RCMP uniform. Maddie noticed his sergeant badge, three yellow chevrons and a crown for the first time. She had been so mad she couldn't remember if she'd said how proud of her dad she was for earning the promotion, even if it meant moving.

"We're on the bus route," her dad went on. "And you'll get picked up and dropped off at the end of the driveway. If you want to stay later, Mom or I will come and get you until you get your driver's license."

The high school on Douglas Avenue wasn't as small as Maddie had thought, but it was nowhere near as big as Burnaby South. "You're in all of the courses you wanted to take," Dad said. "They don't offer Spanish in the school. But the district has a great online program and we enrolled you in that. Give it a try and if it doesn't work, the counsellor said the two of you will figure something out."

Maddie Joins the Stars

Fort St. James was small and Maddie was still angry about having to move. But she felt a tiny bit better when they stopped at the Fort Forum, the town's hockey rink. The arena looked like almost any other rink she had played in. Maddie liked the feel of it, and was even happier to see that the ice had already been put in.

There was something about a fresh sheet of ice that made Maddie feel better. She was also impressed with the dozens of regional and provincial championship banners hanging from the rafters, and what seemed like a hundred trophies in the cases that lined the foyer and the walkway at the top of the bleachers. Clearly hockey was a big thing here.

"Teams from the Fort are called the Stars," Dad added. "Their colours are green, black and white. The Fort St. James Stars have won provincial championships at every level from Peewee to Midget. Four locals have even gone on to play in the NHL. The town is crazy about hockey."

"But they don't have a girls' team at Bantam, do they?" Maddie knew that fact already but it was supported by the team pictures in the trophy cases.

"This is the twenty-first century," a new voice said. "Maybe in the 1980s it was a big thing for a girl to want to play with the boys. Once upon a time a girl playing on a boys' team could have been a book or even a movie! Now? Girl, boy, white, blue or purple. It doesn't matter who you are, as long as you can play. You won't be the first girl to play Bantam or even Midget with the boys. And you won't be the last."

A man walked up to them from out of the players' tunnel. He was wearing blue jeans and a ball cap. He was tall and well-built, his brown hair almost down to his shoulders.

"You must be Sergeant Snow," the man said, shaking Maddie's dad's hand. "We've talked a few times on the phone. It's nice to meet you in person. Welcome to the Fort. And you must be Madeline," he added, shaking Maddie's hand as well. "I've heard a lot of good things about you."

"Maddie, this is Billy Playford, the coach of the Bantam Stars," her dad explained.

"Nice to meet you," Maddie said.

"Your timing is pretty good," said Coach Playford. "We aren't starting practice officially for another month. But I wanted to give the team a chance to shake off the rust so I booked the ice for stick-and-puck for two weeks. You don't have to practise, but it would be a good thing for you to come out and give the guys a chance to get to know you. Some of them are working and others are on holiday, but I figure five or six members of the team will show up tonight."

"I'll be here." The thought of being on the ice made Maddie feel better than she had since goalie camp.

Coach Playford was happy about the answer. "Great. These guys have been playing with each other since kindergarten. You know what small towns are like. We don't get many newcomers and sometimes it takes people a while to fit in."

"You sure you're okay with a girl trying out?" Maddie asked. She actually didn't know what small towns were like, but she certainly felt like an outsider.

"Nobody on the team will care as long as you can stop pucks. And no tryout is required. As soon as your dad called me and said you were moving to the Fort, I did my research. I've watched some of your games on YouTube. You came in second place last season. You're an excellent goalie. Welcome to the Stars."

"For real?" Her dad had said she would have a chance to play, but Maddie hadn't really believed him.

"For real, Maddie. A young man named Connor Spencer has been our number one goalie for the past three years. You'll have to fight to see who starts, but you'll both enjoy the competition, I'm sure. Our other goalie moved to Prince George over the summer and we were starting to panic. It's not easy finding a new goalie at this level."

"I can beat this Connor guy," Maddie said confidently. "I've started my entire career."

Coach Playford grinned. "That's the spirit. He won't be back in town for a couple of weeks, but you can bet he'll hear about you soon enough. And don't forget to bring all your gear," he said. "It might be just stick-and-puck, but the guys will want to test you."

★★★

"You sure you're okay?" Maddie's dad asked her as they loaded her gear into the truck. The Snows had an early dinner so Maddie wouldn't have to play on a full stomach, but Maddie had hardly touched her food. For the first time in years she was nervous about playing.

"I'm fine," she said, climbing up into the passenger seat.

"Good," her dad replied as he drove out of the driveway. "You'll do great."

It took less than ten minutes to drive the six kilometres to the rink. Back in Burnaby, travelling the same distance would have taken at least twice that, even more in rush hour. But from the look of the number of cars on the road, Maddie guessed that Fort St. James had never heard of rush hour.

Maddie's dad pulled to a stop in front of the Fort Forum. "I'm going to go to the detachment to get a little work done. I'll be back just after eight. I'll wait outside for you."

"Great." Maddie went to the back of the truck and pulled out her heavy bag. "And dad," she added, "thanks for the ride."

"You're welcome." Her dad smiled as he started up the truck engine. "Now get in there and show these small-town boys what a big-city girl can do!"

7 A BIG SURPRISE

"Maddie, welcome!" said Coach Playford as Maddie entered the rink. "It's six-thirty. Good to see you here early. I like players to be punctual."

"I wanted to give myself time to change," she said. "Before . . ." She didn't need to finish the sentence.

"Don't worry, Maddie, I've got a dressing room reserved for you. You'll have it all to yourself."

Maddie followed Coach Playford to the dressing room. She felt very strange dressing without anyone else there. Getting ready for a game or a practice was usually a very social time. She liked to talk to her friends, to get caught up on whatever drama was going on in their lives. To get on her gear alone was unsettling. With no distractions, it only took her a few minutes to dress.

"You were quick," said Coach Playford as Maddie came out of her dressing room. "The rest of the team takes forever to get ready."

Maddie noticed that he had put his skates on. In

shoes her new coach was a tall man. In skates? He looked like a giant.

Maddie made her way through the tunnel to the players' bench. Behind her she heard the sound of voices and laughter. It was the rest of the team, old friends lacing up their skates, getting ready to play together for the thousandth time.

Maddie opened the gate, stepped out onto the ice and glided to the nearest net. "All right posts," she said quietly, tapping the goalposts, left, right, left. "Don't let me down. I'm going to need your help so I don't make a fool of myself."

The first skater on the ice was Coach Playford himself. Billy Playford was a big man at least her dad's age, but Maddie was amazed at how quickly and gracefully he skated. He moved across the ice without effort. Maddie was a good skater, but compared to him she felt like a beginner. The rest of the team, the ones who were in town anyway, followed Coach Playford out. They skated over to say hi to their coach. And to her.

"I'd like to introduce Madeline Snow," Coach Playford said. The boys were leaning on their sticks, standing in a semi-circle around Maddie and the coach. "She's good, believe me. She's going to give Connor a run for his money when it comes to starting position."

One by one the boys introduced themselves. "I'm Justin," said a blonde boy with just the beginnings of a faint mustache. "I'm the captain. Nice to have you on the team."

"Gabriel," said the next, a large boy with dark hair and eyes. "Welcome to the Fort."

"I'm Branden."

"Drew."

"Ryan."

"Jag."

"Aidan."

"Marco."

"Daniel."

Each boy in turn skated up and said hello.

"All right, everyone," said Coach Playford. "Let's get started. Madeline, stretch and get ready. I'm going to lead the boys in a little skate around the rink. Then we'll play some three-on-three."

With Coach Playford in the lead, the boys skated around the rink, first slowly, then picking up speed. They moved from lazy arcs to tight circles, frontwards, backwards, then frontwards again.

"Hey Madeline, do you mind if I stretch with you? My hamstring is acting up a bit."

"Sure," said Maddie as Aidan, a tall, red-haired boy glided toward her. She was down on her knees stretching out her calves. "And call me Maddie. Coach Playford is a great skater," she said to her new teammate as they stretched.

"He better be," Aidan said. "He's a legend, after all."

"Legend?"

Aidan looked at her with surprise. "Seriously? You don't know who Billy Playford is? I thought you were from the city, not outer space!"

"What are you talking about?" Maddie was more confused than ever.

"First round of the draft in 1992? Are you saying you don't know who he is?"

The year Aidan mentioned was a long time before Maddie was born. But all of a sudden, things were making sense as something clicked in her memory.

"Coach won two Stanley Cups with the Penguins," said Aidan. "He was on track for a Hall of Fame career until he went hard into the boards in a game against the Bruins. Hurt his leg bad. MCL, ACL — you name it. Whatever parts of your knee can get wrecked got wrecked."

"That's awful," Maddie said.

"Coach tried to come back but things were too badly damaged. He retired from the league at twenty-six."

"So what's he doing here? In the Fort, I mean?"

"He was born here," Aidan answered. "The Playfords own a logging company. They've been here for like a hundred years. The elementary school in town is even named after his grandfather. When he retired from hockey, Coach came home to work in the family business, but he still loves hockey. He's been the Bantam Stars coach for years."

"That is so cool." Maddie had met a few NHL players before, but never one who had won two Stanley Cups.

"He doesn't talk about it much," Aidan said. "He's pretty modest."

"Doesn't talk much about what?" Coach Playford asked, sliding to a stop in front of Maddie and Aidan.

"Your haircut, Coach!" Aidan said. "The '80s are over. Time to get rid of the mullet."

"Very funny, Mr. Benedict," said Coach Playford. "Just wait until I make you do sprints. I'll be the one laughing then."

The rest of the boys gathered round Coach Playford when he blew his whistle. "Okay boys, let's welcome our new goalie to the team with a little game of half-ice three-on-three. Aidan, Justin and Gabriel. You start on defence. Ready? Let's go!"

Coach Playford reached into the pocket of his hoody and tossed a puck down the ice. Maddie watched as it skittered toward the centre line. Like they'd done it a thousand times before, the boys skated into position.

"Here comes the first goal," said Drew, a strong-looking Indigenous player who wore his black hair long. He skated quickly to the puck and took it expertly with the blade of his stick. He turned in a tight circle and skated full speed toward the net.

Branden and Jag fell in beside him, Branden on the left wing, Jag on the right. Gabriel, Justin and Aidan squared up to face them, protecting Maddie and the net.

A Big Surprise

Focus.

Suddenly everything else went away. Her anger at the move, her sadness about leaving her team and her friends. Everything disappeared as Maddie settled into her stance. All that mattered was the player coming toward her.

Ryan crossed the blue line. She watched as he lifted his stick as if to shoot a slapshot. She felt her muscles tense, ready to spring.

Instead of shooting, Ryan faked. He slid the puck to Branden on his left. Maddie quickly moved, adjusting her body to face Branden. Aidan skated over to try to stop him but Branden snapped the puck almost as soon as he took the pass.

Focus.

Even with Aidan in the way, Maddie picked up the puck as it flew off the blade of Branden's stick. She moved her right arm and felt the puck slam into her blocker. She heard the thud it made and watched from the side of her mask as it bounced up into the netting behind the boards and out of play.

"Great save!" one of the boys shouted.

"She stoned you, Branden!" laughed another one.

"Good stop," said Coach Playford skating over to Maddie. "I think you have their attention now. Let's see what else you can do."

They played three-on-three for the next forty minutes. The boys took turns on offence and defence. More than a few pucks got past Maddie. But she made half a dozen or more great saves, including one on a shot from Coach Playford himself. She snagged the puck out of mid-air with her glove, to the cheers of her new team.

By the end of the practice Maddie was tired, sweaty and sore. But she was happier than she'd been in weeks. It felt good to be back on the ice and even better to be welcomed and cheered by her new teammates. Maybe, just maybe, she wouldn't be running back to Burnaby after all.

At least not yet.

8 The FIRST DAY OF SCHOOL

By the beginning of September, Maddie had met all the players on the Fort St. James Stars except for Connor Spencer, the team's other goalie. Connor had been on holiday with his parents and would be back for the first day of school. But as Maddie walked into Fort St. James Secondary School, her stomach full of butterflies, she had other things on her mind.

Maddie's old school, Burnaby South Secondary School, had 1,800 students. It was so huge that Maddie didn't know half of the students in her own grade, let alone the rest of the school. Fort St. James Secondary had fewer than 400 students. To Maddie, it felt a bit like a middle school.

Everyone knew each other, Maddie could tell. She saw some of the boys she knew from the Stars. They said hello to her but they were busy with their own friends.

"Excuse me, do you know where Ms. Thompson's room is?" Maddie asked an Indigenous girl with a nice smile and long black hair. Maddie had stopped at the office to pick up her schedule. Even though the school was small she didn't know where any of her classes were. First up was English 9.

"Down the second-floor hall, third room on the left," said the girl. "I'm in that class too. I'll show you the way."

"Thanks," Maddie said. "I'm new here."

"Your name is Madeline, right? Your dad is the new sergeant and you're a goalie on the Stars."

"Maddie, actually. But how did you know that?" Maddie had never seen this girl in her life but whoever she was, she seemed to know a lot about Maddie.

"We're a small town. People know everything about everyone else. Get used to it. Besides, my cousin Gabriel is on your hockey team. My name's Emma," the girl said. "Emma Prince. The Fort's not a bad place, but it is different from the city."

Maddie could see some of the differences in the faces of the students they passed on their way to Ms. Thompson's English class. Burnaby South was full of students from all over the world. It was one of the most multicultural schools in the country. But the students here in Fort St. James were almost all Indigenous or white, with only a handful of South Asian and Chinese-Canadians.

"Welcome back, everyone," said Ms. Thompson when the bell rang and students took their seats. She was a middle-aged lady with round glasses. To Maddie's surprise, Ms. Thompson spoke with an English accent.

"And welcome to Fort St. James, Ms. Snow," the teacher added to Maddie. "I'm sure you will do just fine here."

After English class, it was time for Math class. After Math came lunch. When she sat down by herself in the small cafeteria to eat, Maddie suddenly felt lonely. The students were nice enough, but they weren't her old friends. And this wasn't her old school. Any good feelings she'd had playing stick-and-puck disappeared.

"Do you mind if I join you?"

Maddie looked up to see Emma Prince. "Please," Maddie said, grateful for somebody to talk to.

Emma sat across from Maddie at the table and took a bite from her sandwich. "How are you doing?" Emma asked. "I remember my first day in grade four when we moved to Vancouver. I was so scared, I don't know how I survived it."

"You went to school in Vancouver?"

"For four years till the end of grade seven," said Emma. "I was born here. But when I was nine my mom decided to get a degree in Forestry Sciences from UBC. She wanted a better job. I'm Dakelh First Nation, from Nak'azdli Whut'en. The band was encouraging members to upgrade their education so off we went. My mom's now the chief forester for our logging operations."

"Wow. Moving to Vancouver must have been strange," said Maddie. It was weird enough moving from the city to a small town. She couldn't imagine what it would be like the other way around.

"It was terrible at first," said Emma. "We left a big house and moved into a tiny apartment near UBC. All the people, the noise, the buildings. I thought I was going to go crazy. It took me a year to get used to it."

"My first night in the Fort was so quiet I thought I was going crazy." Despite the differences, Maddie knew what Emma was talking about. Moving to a new place was hard. "I didn't realize how used to noise I was in Burnaby."

"I get that. I hated it at first. But things got better when I made some friends and got used to the place," Emma said. "By my third year I was a big-city girl. Going downtown, biking the seawall at Stanley Park, shopping at Pacific Centre and . . ."

"Metro Mall!" both girls said at the same time.

"We could have been in the same store at the same time!" said Maddie.

"And now we are in the same school in the Fort," said Emma. "It took me ages to get used to this place again. But now that I'm back I wouldn't want to be anywhere else."

Before Maddie could say anything else, a voice cut in. "Hey Emma, how was your summer?" A boy their age followed his voice over to their table. He was tall, with curly brown hair and blue eyes.

"Hi Connor," Emma said. "It was fine. Yours?"

"It was awesome. We were in the Okanagan for

most of it. We got back in town last night." The boy looked at Maddie. "You must be Maddie. I've heard a lot about you. The guys say you are pretty good between the pipes." Connor Spencer, the starting goalie of the Fort St. James Stars, shook Maddie's hand. "I'm looking forward to our first practice together."

"So that's the famous Connor Spencer," Maddie whispered to Emma when he left a minute or so later. "People talk about him like he's a movie star."

"Connor's actually a very nice guy. When you get to know him you'll really like him."

There was something in Emma's tone that made Maddie smile. "You sound like you really like him already. Anything you want to tell me?"

Emma laughed. "We're just friends. For Connor, his family and hockey come first."

"People say he's a really good goalie. How good?"

"Good enough to be drafted by the Trail Smoke Eaters when he was thirteen. He was supposed to play Junior A in Trail this year, but his mom got breast cancer so he stayed home. The nearest cancer clinic is in Prince George and he wanted to be around to help look after his little sister."

"How's his mom now?" Maddie didn't want to like Connor. He was her competition for the starting goalie job. It would have been easier for Maddie to want to beat him if Connor was a bit of a jerk, like some really good athletes were. But to find out he put off going to play junior hockey to look after his family? That was something only a really nice person would do.

"She's fine now," Emma said. "This is Connor's last year with the Stars. He'll be joining the Smoke Eaters next season. And then? Major Junior for sure. Maddie, you'll have the chance to start next year, but for now, if I were you, I'd get used to being the backup goalie. Nice guy or not, Connor won't let anyone take the starting position from him without a fight."

9 THE LAKE

Before Maddie knew it, almost a full month had gone by. She made new friends, but she also kept in touch with her old friends and teammates on social media. Maddie was getting used to her new home. But her worst day in weeks was when she saw a picture on Instagram of the Wildcats at their first practice, with April starting in net instead of her.

"Are you okay, Maddie?" her mom asked. Maddie had been sitting on the couch in the living room, chatting on her phone when she saw the picture. Her face flushed and tears started flowing. It felt like she'd been hit in the stomach by a puck.

"I'm fine," was all Maddie managed to say before running downstairs to her room. She slammed the door shut and threw herself onto the bed. It was hours until she felt okay enough to leave her room.

Even though Maddie had met all the boys on the team, including Connor Spencer, she hadn't seen Connor play. She had heard the stories about what a good player Connor was, and found herself both nerv-ous and excited about it. She loved competition. She wasn't about to give the starting job to Connor no matter how good or how nice he was. She was good as well, and she would try her best to win the position.

***

Before the first full practice of the season, Maddie got an invitation from Emma Prince. "Hey, Maddie," Emma said during English class on a Friday. "My mom wants to know if you're interested in going out on Stuart Lake with us tomorrow when we pull in our salmon nets."

"In a boat?" Maddie asked.

Emma laughed. "Of course in a boat! What do you think we'd take on the lake? A helicopter?"

"Sure, that would be awesome," Maddie said. "I've never been on a boat before, except for ferry rides to Vancouver Island for hockey tournaments."

"Never? Are you serious?" It looked like Emma could hardly believe what her friend had said. "We live on the water up here."

"Well," Maddie said, "I went on *Pirates of the Caribbean* at Disney but that's about it."

"Then I'm glad you're coming tomorrow," Emma said. "Be at my house at eight in the morning. And wear something warm," she added. "It's almost October. It's going to be really cold out there."

The Lake

★★★

"Welcome to our home, Maddie," Emma's mom said the next morning. Maddie and her dad were right on time at Emma's house, a small split-level in Nak'azdli, just up from Stuart Lake. "I'm Anna Prince. And welcome to Fort St. James, Sergeant Snow. I've heard some good things about you already."

"We're happy to be part of the community," Maddie's dad said. "What time should I come and get Maddie?"

"No need for that," Anna said. "I'll drive her home after lunch if that works for you."

"That would be very nice," her dad said, climbing back into his truck. "Make sure you wear a life jacket, Maddie. You're a good swimmer but that water's a lot colder than the pool at Bonsor or Edmonds Community Centre."

As Anna, Emma and Maddie walked down to the lake, Anna said, "My daughter says you've never been in a real boat before." They stopped beside a long boat pulled up onto the shore.

"It's true I'm afraid," Maddie replied. "I guess I never had the chance back home."

"I really liked living in the city," Emma said. "But catching salmon was one of the things I missed the most when I was at school. *Dakelh* in our language means 'people who travel by boat.' And that is who we are. Being on the water is in our blood."

Anna took life jackets out of the boat and passed them to the girls. "Put this on, Maddie," she said. "Your dad is right. The water's very cold. Good swimmer or not, you wouldn't last five minutes in the water without this."

Anna untied the boat from a log. With the girls helping, she pushed it into the water. The bottom slid easily over the gravel beach. "Hop in," she said. "Time to get some salmon."

Maddie and Emma sat next to each other as Anna started the outboard motor. The boat slowly putted out into the still grey water. "The Europeans named this lake Stuart, after one of their own," Anna explained, "but the Dakelh have called it *Nakal Bun* for centuries. That mountain over there, the one with the large bald face? Do you see it?"

"Of course," said Maddie. The mountain was the most noticeable feature about the town, a large form with a huge bare limestone patch surrounded by trees. "That's Mount Pope. Our house is by it."

"Europeans called it Pope after a surveyor who came through here a century ago. But we prefer *Nakal Dzulh, Mountain of the Lake*. It's important for our people, for all people actually, to learn the original names of places.

"And soon you're going to learn about salmon, or *talo* in Dakelh!" said Anna. She eased back on the engine as they approached several floats bobbing on the surface of the water.

"We've been netting and smoking salmon forever," Anna said. "Emma's an expert at catching fish. Even when she was little she was better at fishing than I was or even her dad."

"I haven't told Maddie about Dad," Emma said. Maddie noticed her friend's eyes suddenly looked sad. Maddie knew Emma lived with just her mom, and she was too polite to ask about her father.

"He died in an accident when Emma was five," Anna explained. "Nine years ago, he was driving back from a logging camp north of town. It was the middle of the winter. He lost control on the ice and hit a tree. There are many good things about the North. But far too often people die young here. It can be a dangerous place to live."

Anna shut off the engine as they neared the first float. Suddenly all was silent except for the gentle sound of water slapping against the side of the boat.

It was a clear, cold morning. Maddie's breath rose in a mist as she took in the view of the countryside. On the ice, Maddie had always been able to shut out distractions and noise, and there was plenty of both in the city. Here, the silence was almost overwhelming, but, oddly enough, Maddie loved it. There was a sense of peace she never felt in the hustle and bustle of Burnaby. Maybe there were some good things about living in the North.

"Okay girls," said Anna. "Help me pull in the floats. With a bit of luck, the net will be full!"

Maddie leaned over the side of the boat and grabbed the rope tied to the bottom of the float. When she touched the water, a cold chill ran up her arm.

"I told you it was cold," Anna said. "But well worth it if there are salmon."

Maddie and Emma pulled hard on the ropes that seemed to vanish into the dark water. "I think we're in luck," grunted Emma. Whatever was below them in the water was very heavy. Maddie strained, pulling slowly on the rope, the icy water making her hands feel numb.

Suddenly, a silvery flash of movement appeared beneath them. "Definitely in luck!" laughed Anna. "Pull, girls. Get that net into the boat. Grandma's got the smokehouse ready. I don't want to disappoint her!"

It took several more heaves before the net emerged from the lake. Within it were eight, maybe ten, large hump-backed salmon. They were red and silver, with large oddly hooked mouths, their heads and tails almost green.

"Sockeyes," said Anna.

"Those are the ugliest fish I've ever seen!" Maddie said as they pulled the net into the boat. The large salmon, each one of them at least two kilograms, flopped around in the net, slapping their tails against the wooden boat bottom.

"Spawners," said Anna. "In the ocean they are pretty

and silver. When they hit fresh water, they turn this colour and shape. Not so nice to look at but delicious when smoked. There was a time not so long ago when our people's survival depended on catching enough salmon to last through the winter. Their journey from the coast is a miracle of nature."

"Maybe," Maddie said as the fish squirmed around her feet. "But I think I prefer my miracles of nature deep fried or in a sushi roll."

10 THE FIRST PRACTICE

"You're sure you don't want me to watch?" Maddie's dad asked as he dropped her off at the Fort Forum. It was cold for the first day of October, below zero already. A coating of ice covered the puddles in the gravel parking lot of the rink.

"Seriously, Dad?"

Her dad smiled as he lifted Maddie's bag out of the box of his truck. "I get it. I'll be back at nine." Before he could drive away a red Ford pickup pulled up.

"Hey, Maddie! I can't wait to see you play!" Connor Spencer said as he climbed out of the cab of the truck. "Hi Sergeant Snow," Connor said, shaking her dad's hand. "Nice to meet you. This is my dad."

"Good to meet you, Sergeant." Connor's dad got out of the truck and shook her dad's hand as well. "Andy Spencer. Welcome to the Fort."

As their dads talked, Maddie and Connor walked into the rink. "You ready?" Connor asked. "Coach

Playford and Coach Willick are going to put us through our paces pretty hard."

"Who's Coach Willick?" Coach Playford had been the only adult at stick-and-puck.

"Danny Willick is the assistant coach," Connor said. "He played in the AHL for a couple of seasons. Never quite made the big leagues, but he's awesome. I've learned a lot from him. You will too."

"Maddie, you have the dressing room on the left," said Coach Playford when they walked into the tunnel. "Get ready and hit the ice."

"See you out there, Maddie," Connor said. He entered the main dressing room with the rest of the team while Maddie got dressed alone. It was still strange to Maddie to be changing by herself. It was lonely. She missed the laughs and the joking around with the rest of the team.

★★★

"Okay everyone, let's get started." Coach Playford and another man stepped onto the ice to join the players. Coach Willick was shorter and smaller than Coach Playford, with blonde curly hair. But as Maddie watched him expertly skate in loops around the rink she could tell he knew what he was doing.

They started with stretches, followed by skating drills. Connor was right. Coach Playford didn't mess around when it came to practices. Even Maddie and Connor, dressed in their goalie equipment, were expected to skate hard. Soon Maddie was soaked in sweat.

"Goalies, go with Coach Willick," Coach Playford said when the skating stopped. "Skaters. Two lines on the blue line. Cycle, give and go."

Maddie and Connor skated to the far net as the rest of the team started cycling through their drill.

"Welcome to the team, Maddie," said Coach Willick. "Okay you two. Show me your stances."

Assuming the proper stance was a goaltending basic Maddie had learned as a child. She set her feet apart, skates parallel to each other. Her knees were forward and slightly bent. Shoulders square, stick on ice, glove out and open. Maddie caught with her left hand and held her stick in her right. Connor was bigger and Maddie saw he caught with his right hand.

"Excellent, both of you," said Coach Willick. "Now, T push."

The T push was how goalies move from side to side in the net. Maddie pushed hard with her right leg and slid quickly to the left. She quickly got back into her stance then pushed back to the right.

"Good." Coach Willick seemed impressed.

You should be, Maddie thought. She had been playing goal for eight years.

Coach Willick ran them through drills. Shuffling, C cuts, butterfly and recovery. All the while Maddie kept an eye on Connor, watching how he was doing. From what she saw he was doing very well.

"You know your stuff, Maddie," said Connor.

"So do you," she replied.

Connor seemed to move effortlessly. All they were doing was positioning drills, but Maddie could tell he was good. She was curious to see how good he would be with pucks flying in the air toward him. She would soon have that chance.

"Get a drink," Coach Willick said. "Shooting drills are next."

"Connor, you go first," Coach Playford said after the break. Maddie skated to the side boards and watched as the rest of the team lined up on the blue line.

The drill was simple. Coach Playford dumped a bucket of pucks onto the ice. The players lined up in a half circle between the crease and the blue line and would take turns shooting at the goalie.

"You start, Aidan," Coach Playford said. "One shot at a time. Let the goalie recover and try to keep the pucks low. We don't need any concussions in the first practice of the year."

"You got it, Coach," Aidan said. He shot a hard slapshot that stayed low on the ice. Connor shot out his stick and stopped the puck easily.

One after the other, the boys took their turn. Some tried slapshots, shooting as hard as they could. Others took wrist shots or snapshots. Some tried deking Connor out. One after the other, Connor stopped almost all of them. He used his pads, his blocker, his stick and his glove, quickly getting back into position after each shot.

In total only three shots got past Connor. Two wristers went high blocker side into the top of the net. A booming slapshot from Gabriel went five hole. Connor almost saved that one, but the puck ricocheted off the side of his skate and slid into the net through his pads.

"You're up, Maddie."

Maddie had been watching Connor make stop after stop. He was very good. She was nervous and excited at the same time. The boys shot much harder than most of the girls she'd played against, but she felt sure she could handle it.

Maddie took her place in the net. She tapped her posts like she always did — left, right, left. Then she got into position.

Focus.

"Branden, you start." Coach Playford blew his whistle. As he did, Branden leaned into his stick and fired a wicked snapshot. Before Maddie could even see it she heard the sound of the frozen rubber clanging into the metal goalpost on her glove side.

"So close!" Branden groaned at missing the goal by less than a centimetre.

"Thank you posts," Maddie whispered, shaking off the near miss. It would have been awful to get scored on with the very first shot against her.

Gabriel was next. *These guys can shoot*, Maddie thought. She would have to concentrate like never before. *He's going to slap it*, she told herself.

Sure enough, Gabriel tried a slapshot. The puck skittered over the ice toward the net, but Maddie had it all the way. She moved her stick and made the save, watching the puck fly off the blade and into the bleachers.

"Great save!" shouted Coach Willick.

Drew was next. His shot was a wrist shot high to the stick side. Maddie slid slightly to the left and angled her blocker, grunting a little when the puck slammed into it. *That was a hard shot!*

Ryan was the first one to score on Maddie. He snapped the puck right through the gap between Maddie's catching hand and her body.

Maddie cursed. It was a perfectly placed shot. Almost no one could have saved it. But she didn't like getting scored on at any time, let alone when she was trying to earn the starting goalie position.

Focus.

She got back into her stance and shut out everything except Paul. His shot was a rocket. But Maddie read it all the way, snagging it in mid-air to the cheers of the team.

Half an hour later, after Maddie had faced dozens of shots, Coach Playford split the team in two. The fifteen minute scrimmage ended 2–2. When Coach Playford blew the final whistle and the Fort St. James Stars skated off the ice, Maddie was exhausted and covered in sweat. But she was happier than she'd been for weeks.

Maddie had more than held her own. Connor Spencer was a terrific goalie but Maddie had shown her new team she wasn't going to settle for the position of backup goalie without a fight. The first game was three weeks away. She had plenty of time to prove she deserved to be the number one goalie.

11 DINNER WITH A RIVAL

The first game of the season was set for the second Saturday in November, and Maddie did everything she could to be ready for it. Practice after practice, she worked harder than she ever had before, stopping puck after puck until her entire body ached.

Off the ice she practised hard as well. She lifted weights in the school's small gym after classes. She ran outside until the cold weather and the ice, now nearly constant on the roads, forced her inside to the treadmill her dad had bought for them.

Hard work and practice aside, Maddie was uneasy knowing that Connor was better than she was. It wasn't just that he was bigger. Connor moved faster than any goalie she'd seen, sticking out his stick or his glove to make stops that almost seemed impossible.

If Connor had been a jerk, it would have been easy for Maddie to be jealous and dislike him. But the truth was that Connor was one of the nicest people she'd met since moving to the Fort. Maddie learned just how nice Connor was when she was invited to his place for dinner.

"My mom wants to meet you," Connor said. "Come around three and bring skates. Regular skates, not goalie skates if you want. We have a tennis court that we flood every winter. We can skate and shoot around. Sometimes it's nice to be on the ice without all that padding, right?"

Maddie's dad dropped her off at Connor's house the Saturday afternoon before their first game. Like the Snows, the Spencers lived near the shores of Stuart Lake. But Connor's house was to the west, about ten kilometres out of town.

"You have an awesome place," said Maddie as Connor showed her around. Their house was made of logs, like Maddie's, but it was much bigger. There were garages and outbuildings with large pieces of logging equipment and trucks stored in them, or parked neatly to the side.

"Welcome, Maddie," said Connor's mom. "Connor's told us so many great things about you that we just had to have you over."

"He did, Mrs. Spencer?" Maddie was surprised to catch Connor blushing, just a bit.

"He did." Connor's mom said as she smiled. "And please, call me Eileen."

"I'm glad you brought your skates, Maddie," Connor said, cutting in before his mom could embarrass him again. "I'll show you our rink. We have an hour before it gets dark. We can skate around for a bit then go in for some hot chocolate."

"Sound good to me," Maddie replied. She was glad she had brought the regular skates from her power skating classes in Burnaby instead of her goalie skates. Maddie's goalie skates were covered with plastic shields. The blades were longer and thicker than those of her regular skates, and her feet sat lower. They were great for stopping pucks, but not so good for skating.

"This is the earliest we've flooded the tennis court in ages," Connor said. They sat on a bench beside the rink, tying up their skates. It had been ages since Maddie had worn regular skates. They felt lighter than her goalie stakes, like wearing a pair of sneakers after walking around in hiking boots.

"It is pretty cold." Maddie's breath rose as steam when she spoke. For the past week, the temperature had been around ten degrees below zero, more than enough for a thick coat of ice to freeze on the concrete surface of the court. "The rink looks great," Maddie added. There were regulation nets on either side of the rink. Somebody had even painted red, blue and crease lines onto the concrete.

"My grandpa says it's gonna be a long, cold winter, one of the worst in years. So much for global warming," Connor said, stepping onto the ice. "He's normally right about that sort of thing. He's lived here for seventy-five years."

Connor leaned over the boards and grabbed two sticks from a barrel beside the rink. "Left-handed for you and right for me," he said.

Maddie took the stick he handed her and glided onto the ice. The surface was a little rough but more than good enough for skating.

Maddie could already tell that November in the North was very different from late fall in Metro Vancouver. In Burnaby, it got cold from time to time, and windshields and lawns sometimes got a coating of frost. But mostly it was rainy. Some trees lost their leaves but many didn't. Even in January there was always lots of greenery.

In the Fort? Autumn had been beautiful, with the trees covered in beautiful shades of yellow and red. But it had been short. Now, winter was here. Except for the spruce, fir and pine trees, every bush and tree was stripped of their leaves. They looked dead to Maddie.

The sky was often cloudy here as well. But the edges of Stuart Lake were coated with ice, and frost was a constant feature. With the snowline creeping down the mountains, the country looked like it was slowly being covered by a large grey blanket.

"Six months of winter to go," Connor said. He dropped a puck onto the ice and passed it to Maddie with a gentle flick of his stick. "Thank goodness we have hockey."

They played for nearly an hour, passing the puck back and forth, shooting into the net. They talked all the while. It felt good to Maddie to be free of her gear, to skate and play and move quickly over the ice.

By the time they took off their skates, the sun had dipped below the mountains at the far end of the lake. Shadows grew long and dark on the ice. "I don't know about you, but I'm ready for the fire and a cup of hot chocolate," Connor said. "Food too. My mom's making her world-famous chicken pie for dinner. I hope you like it."

Maddie was starving. "Don't worry about that," she said, following Connor off the ice. "I'm so hungry I could eat a live chicken right now!"

★★★

"So how do you like the Fort so far?" asked Eileen Spencer as they sat down to eat in the large dining room.

"It's taking some getting used to," Maddie said honestly between mouthfuls of chicken pie. Connor's worry that Maddie wouldn't like his mom's cooking was quickly put to rest when Maddie started eating.

"And how do you *like* Connor?" giggled Sarah, Connor's ten-year-old sister, from across the table.

"That's enough, young lady. You don't need to embarrass our guest," said Andy Spencer. Connor's dad had a smile on his lips.

"We're just friends and teammates," Connor told his little sister. "You say sorry."

"It's okay," Maddie said. She quite liked Sarah. The girl was funny and talkative. She reminded Maddie a little of herself when she was that age.

"How are you feeling about the game tomorrow?" Eileen asked, giving Maddie a second slice of pie.

"Most likely I won't be playing," she said. "Coach Playford's set the lineup and Connor is starting." Maddie had been a little upset about that at first. The Stars opened the season against the Bears in Vanderhoof. Maddie had worked hard, harder than ever. But this would be the first game in ages she hadn't started.

"You never know," Connor said. "Our games against Vanderhoof are pretty chippy, even for Bantam. More than a few players, goalies included, have been hurt on the ice. I might be starting, but there's no guarantee I'll finish."

"Vanderhoof and Fort St. James have been bitter rivals for years," explained Andy. "We just don't like each other. When I played, there were fights, even bench-clearing brawls on a regular basis. I'm just glad the Minor Hockey Association has banned fighting now. Too many people used to get hurt. Mind you, it does happen from time to time when tempers flare."

"Grandpa says the same thing," Connor said to Maddie. "He played hockey for the Fort as well, back around the time of the Second World War. He played on the old outside rink the town had before the Forum was built. But the rivalry between Fort St. James and

Vanderhoof is even older. It has been going on for a hundred years or more."

"Wow," Maddie said. "I knew hockey was important in the Fort. But I didn't know just how serious you all are about it."

"I can't explain it to you," Connor said, "but believe me, when the puck drops next Saturday in Vanderhoof, you'll see exactly what I'm talking about."

12 THE VANDERHOOF BEARS

Maddie had never seen so many people at a Bantam hockey game. The Vanderhoof arena was full of cheering Bears fans. There were 400 of them at least. Sitting behind the visiting Stars' bench were fifty or so parents from the Fort. Her mom and dad were up there as well, sitting next to Connor's parents.

The atmosphere was tense. The Stars skated onto the rink to warm up and were booed louder than Maddie had ever heard. The only sound louder than the boos was the cheer that filled the rink when the Vanderhoof Bears came onto the ice.

The Stars wore their away greens with a white star and white and black trim. Maddie liked her new jersey. But she had to admit that it felt a little strange after wearing the black and red of the Wildcats for so long.

What was even stranger was the new number on Maddie's back. "You can't have number one, I'm afraid," Coach Playford had told her as he handed Maddie her team jersey. "Connor wears that number. We have thirty-one for you instead. That's Carey Price's number. It's a great one for goalies."

With her new jersey and number on her back, Maddie joined the rest of the team as they huddled up next to their bench.

"Okay, everyone," said Coach Playford. "You all know the history here. This is going to be a Boston–Montreal, original six kind of thing. It's going to be a grinder. I don't want to lose to these guys. But don't forget what happened last spring in the play-offs. I don't want to see a repeat of that, understand? Play tough but disciplined."

"What happened last spring?" Maddie asked Gabriel as Connor and the starting line were taking their positions on the ice.

"We were up by three goals with just a couple of minutes left," Gabriel said. He took his seat next to Maddie on the bench. "It was a gong show. The game was over and we were going to the provincials. Then number fourteen, a goon on the Bears named Willy Jack, decided to take a run at Connor. He hit him from behind. Connor's head hit the crossbar of the net."

"Was he okay?" Maddie asked. Taking a dirty hit and going headfirst into the iron was every goalie's worst nightmare.

"He was fine," said Gabriel. "But he could have been really hurt. One of the guys on the team dropped his gloves to show Willy what happens when he gives our goalie a cheap shot."

"I thought fighting was banned."

"It is. But that didn't stop us. A few gross misconducts and a dozen match penalties later the game ended. We won, but five of us were suspended for the first two games of the playoffs. We were lucky to make it to the provincials."

"Who dropped the gloves first?"

Gabriel smiled. "I did. I think most of the boos you heard were for me. I've not been very popular in Vanderhoof since then."

Maddie was surprised. She could easily believe Drew and Branden would be involved in something like that. They were tough and played with a real edge. But not Gabriel. "You're not a fighter, are you?"

Gabriel was one of Maddie's best friends on the team. He was big for his age. But he was an even-tempered quiet boy who liked to read. And Maddie knew he was one of the best students in grade nine.

"No. I hardly believed it myself afterward. But you do what you have to do to look after your teammates."

For the first time in years, Maddie watched the game start from the bench. The game was tough from the opening puck drop.

Justin, the centre on the first line and Stars number seventeen, won the face-off. He flicked the puck back to Drew, the left wing. Like a shot Drew was off toward the Bears' net with Justin and Branden in support.

Bears' defender number twenty-one lowered his shoulder to Drew. The hit was clean but hard. Bears fans cheered as Drew went heavily into the boards, but not before dishing the puck to Justin, who flicked it over to Branden.

Standing at the hash marks, Justin fired a heavy one-timer toward the Bears net. The puck went high and over the goalie's glove. It rang off the iron and into the netting behind the net. Oohs and ahhs came from the large crowd.

"Great start, team!" yelled Coach Playford from the bench. The teams changed lines and the players lined up in the Bears zone for the face-off.

The first goal came just a few second later. Vanderhoof forward number six won the draw and dropped the puck back to number seventeen, a defender. Aidan stepped heavily into number seventeen, knocking him off the puck.

Then Aidan slapped the puck across the face of the goal to Gabriel. The Bears' goalie was out of position. He scrambled back to face Gabriel, but Gabriel was too fast. With a tap, he put the puck into the back of the net. Stars 1, Bears 0.

A loud chorus of boos rose from the Bears fans as Gabriel skated back to the bench, high-fiving his team. "That's how you do it," Coach Willick said, slapping Gabriel on the back.

Halfway through the first period the Fort scored again. Daniel intercepted a pass around the centre line. Jag, a South Asian player for the Stars, sped down the boards on the right side of the rink. Daniel saw him and fed him a beautiful pass.

Jag picked up the pass at full speed and deked around a Vanderhoof defenceman. With a nifty move, he faked out the Bears' goalie, sending him sprawling to the left.

With a wide-open net in front of him, Jag back-handed the puck into the goal. The Fort parents cheered loudly, though they were drowned out by the shouts and boos of the Vanderhoof fans.

By the middle of the third period the score was 3–1 for the Fort St. James Stars. There had been no fights, though several players from both teams ended up in the penalty box for slashing and roughing.

Connor had made several amazing saves, including one on a penalty shot. Willy Jack, Bears number four-teen, the player Gabriel had fought the season before, was taken down on a breakaway by Ryan. It was a pen-alty to be sure, with Ryan jamming his stick between Willy Jack's legs.

The Vanderhoof players and fans howled with an-ger, though the boos turned to cheers when the ref signalled a penalty shot.

"You can do it, Connor!" Coach Playford cheered from the bench as Willy Jack lined up to take the shot.

Maddie watched closely. She followed fourteen

as he picked up the puck and skated toward Connor. *What's he going to do?* she thought. *Stick side? Backhand? Five-hole?*

From the bench Maddie had watched all the Bears players carefully. Her ability to read the opposition was one of the things that made her a good goalie. Willy Jack was tough and a decent enough player. But she could see he wasn't as good with his hands as some of the other Bears.

Low stick side, for sure, Maddie thought. She watched Willy Jack pick up speed. That's what she would prepare for if she was in the net.

Clearly, Connor thought so as well. Sure enough, after an obvious fake to the glove side, Willy Jack pulled the puck back and tried to shovel it under Connor's stick. Connor had it all the way, poking it easily away toward the boards.

With two minutes to go and the Stars still up by two, the Vanderhoof Bears pulled their goalie. For almost ninety seconds all six Bears on the ice put heavy pressure on the Stars, with most of the play around Connor's crease. It looked like the Bears were going to break through and get another goal. But then Gabriel slid onto the ice, fearlessly blocking a slapshot.

The puck ricocheted off Gabriel's shin pad right toward Drew. Drew crossed his own blue line and with all the Bears chasing him, slid the puck down the ice. Drew was more than thirty metres away from the empty net when he shot. But his aim was perfect. The entire Stars bench cheered as the puck glided over the goal line. With fifteen seconds left it was Fort St. James 4, Vanderhoof 1.

The ref dropped the puck at centre ice. Justin won the face-off and shot it into the corner by the Vanderhoof net. Maddie watched the last few seconds tick off the clock. Then she joined the rest of the team cheering in victory.

Maddie was happy that the Stars won. But inside she felt a little sad. Everyone on the team had been part of the win. Everyone had played. Everyone had skated on the ice.

Everyone except for her.

13 THE REMATCH

The Stars' second game of the season was a rematch against the Vanderhoof Bears, this time in the Fort Forum.

"Check this out, Maddie," said Gabriel as the players lined up in the tunnel. The Bears were already out on the ice.

"Check what out?" Maddie asked.

"Our introduction. It's pretty cool."

Suddenly a loud voice boomed throughout the arena. "Ladies and Gentlemen! It's time for hockey and your Fort St. James Stars!"

Out in the stands the crowd cheered.

"And here's today's starting lineup! At left wing, number twenty-three, Drew Johnson!" Drew stepped quickly onto the ice to the cheers of the crowd.

"At centre, number seventeen, team captain Justin Clarke! At right wing, number nine, Branden McQueen! On defence, number twenty-two, Aidan Benedict! On defence, number seven, Gabriel Prince! In goal, number one, Connor Spencer!"

"That was quite the introduction," Maddie said as she took her spot on the bench.

"That's my uncle Donny," Coach Willick said. "He's been the voice of the Fort Forum for years. He thinks he's Bob Cole or John Shorthouse. He loves to call the games."

The puck dropped and the game began. The Vanderhoof centre won the draw and fed the puck to Willy Jack on right wing. Willy had hardly skated a few metres when he was hit with a thundering body check by Aidan. The home fans roared in approval as Willy Jack fell to the ice.

"I think it's going to be one of those games," said Coach Willick beside Maddie.

Maddie knew exactly what he meant. It would be tough, fast and bruising. At just her second game, she could see how much these two teams didn't like each other.

Halfway through the second period the score was 2–1 for Vanderhoof. The first Bears goal was a brilliant snapshot from just outside the crease. The puck was perfectly placed, flying over Conner's shoulder and into the net.

The second goal was on a wrist shot from the left hash marks that seemed harmless. The puck rose in the air and hit the shaft of a Stars defender, changing its direction. Connor stuck out his glove but misread the puck. He watched helplessly as it flipped end-over-end above his hand and into the net. *I could have saved that*, thought Maddie, watching from the bench.

The score was tied three minutes later on a break-away goal by Justin. The entire bench erupted in cheers along with the fans in the stands. Maddie joined them. But on the inside, she felt anything but happy. She might as well have stayed at home for all she was doing to help the team.

Two quick goals by Gabriel and Ryan in the third period put the game out of reach of the Bears. Connor made some excellent saves, keeping the score at 4–2. The Bears started throwing cheap shots and slashing at sticks. With two minutes to go in the game there was even a fight between Branden and Bears number eleven.

Vanderhoof pulled their goalie, putting an extra skater on the ice in an attempt to tie the game. The Bears pressed hard but couldn't score.

With one minute left Connor made a great save off a hard slapshot. The puck bounced off his stick right to Justin who shovelled it down the ice toward Gabriel. Gabriel took the puck and was about to flash down the ice when Willy Jack cross-checked Marco from behind. Marco went down hard. Before he could get up, Ryan cross-checked Willy Jack, sending him to the ice. Within seconds, players from both teams were pushing each other as the referee and linesmen struggled to pull them apart and keep control.

Maddie wasn't sure what to think. She knew you had to stick up for your teammates. But she'd never seen a hockey fight involving her own team before.

Five minutes later, control was regained. Willy Jack and Ryan were ejected and four more players had penalties.

The ref dropped the puck. The game continued for the few seconds that were left. When the horn blew the crowd erupted in cheers. The Fort St. James Stars won 4–2.

The victory came at a cost.

"Ryan will be suspended for a week," said Coach Willick as they headed to the dressing room. "And Willy Jack from Vanderhoof is looking at two weeks at least."

"How are you feeling, Marco?" Coach Playford asked.

Marco winced. "Shoulder hurts a bit. But I should be fine."

"Get your mom to take you to the doctor to get checked out," Coach Playford instructed. "That was a nasty hit."

Ryan sat on the bench, his nose bloodied from the fight. "Sorry, Coach," he said. "I shouldn't have lost my head like that. You told us to play disciplined and I didn't. I've never been suspended before."

Coach Playford ruffled his hair. "You guys know I don't encourage fighting and that I insist you play fair. But sometimes in the heat of the moment, you do the wrong thing for the right reason. Ryan, you stood up for a teammate. And the Bears will think twice before they play like that again."

★★★

"You don't look happy. What's up?" Emma asked.

The day after the rematch against Vanderhoof, Emma and Maddie were walking downtown for lunch. The day was cold and Maddie was grateful for the warm jacket her mother had bought for her back at Metro Mall.

"I'm a little tired of not playing." Maddie knew about teamwork, about playing your role. But when your role changed from all-star starter to backup, it was a little hard to take.

"Don't worry. You'll get a chance. Your coach isn't going to make you sit on the bench the entire season."

"Maybe," Maddie said glumly.

"Is anything else bothering you?" Emma asked. The girls had become close friends and Emma had never seen Maddie this down.

"Look at this," Maddie said, passing her phone to Emma. "It's my old team's Instagram."

Emma looked through the pictures. The Wildcats had come back champions from a tournament in Abbotsford. Ana Lucia, the goalie who replaced Maddie, was named tournament MVP.

Emma nodded. "That could have been you if you hadn't moved up here."

"It's more than that," Maddie said. "I miss my old friends and my school and my team. Everyone's been nice to me here. But I feel like an outsider, like I don't quite belong."

"There are two kinds of people in the Fort," said Emma slowly. "The Playfords, the Willicks, the Spencers, they've been here for nearly a hundred years. And my people, the Dakelh? We've been here for thousands."

"What about people like me? Newcomers."

"Most of the teachers, doctors, nurses and police move here. Some stay for a long time, but many leave after a couple of years. Some try to fit in, but many don't bother. They think where they were from was better, that they are better than this little northern town."

Maddie felt guilty. She'd judged and made fun of her new home before she'd arrived. "So how does someone like that fit in?" she asked. "How can a person be considered a local?"

Emma put her arm around Maddie as they reached the St. James restaurant. "How do you prepare for games?"

"I don't know," Maddie replied. "I guess I tell myself to focus, to be mindful of nothing but the play around me and to ignore distractions."

"So do that now. Focus on your new town, your new friends and your new team."

"I never thought of it that way." Maddie never

thought about treating life the same way she treated hockey. *It might just work*, she thought.

"That and keep hanging out with an awesome local like me," Emma said. "And when you get your chance to play, show the team how great you are. Nothing makes a person fit into the Fort more than hockey!"

14 Maddie GETS HER CHANCE

Maddie played her first game for the Stars on the last Saturday in November. It was the coldest day of the year so far, almost twenty below zero. A cold northern wind blew snow across the road as Maddie's parents took her to the game in Fraser Lake, a small town a hundred kilometres west.

"Drive slowly," her mom said. "The road looks pretty slick even though it's been sanded."

Early in the week the weather had been cold. But then it had warmed up, almost to five degrees above zero. Some of the snow had melted and they even had rain. But Friday a cold snap blew in from the arctic, dropping the temperature quickly and covering the roads in a sheet of ice. By Saturday morning, crews had salted and sanded the road from Fort St. James but it was still very icy in places.

"Why are we taking the RCMP truck to my game?" Maddie asked.

Instead of driving his new pickup, Maddie's dad had

told her to load her gear into the back of his work truck with the yellow, red and blue RCMP stripe down its white side.

"Because I'm working," her dad explained. "There are lots of accidents on the roads this time of year, especially on a day like this. It's a good thing to have someone patrolling. This way I get to watch you play and do my job."

"If I play." Maddie felt a little better after talking with Emma. But she was still not feeling good about being the backup goalie.

"Don't worry," her dad said. "You'll get your chance. Until then you just have to be patient. You're doing a good job and I love you very much."

Maddie's chance to play came that night. By the end of the first period the Stars were ahead of the Fraser Lake Hawks 5–0.

"They're rebuilding," explained Gabriel as they walked to the dressing room. "Fraser Lake lost twelve players last year to Midget. Most of their team is first year Bantam. They're going to be strong next year, but this season won't be fun for them."

"Maddie," Coach Playford said, "you're in. Time you got your feet wet, don't you think?"

"You'll do great, Maddie," Connor added. "Let's keep that goose egg on the scoreboard. You ready?"

"Ready!" Maddie had been waiting weeks to hear those words. Her heart fluttered a little as she stepped out onto the ice. For the first time, she skated to the net, about to play for the Stars. *Left, right, left.* Maddie tapped the posts gently with her stick. *Focus.*

From the net, she watched the centres take the face-off. Maddie was always a little nervous at the start of a game. This time it was especially true. She hadn't played a real game since spring.

For the next minutes the play was in the Fraser Lake end. The Stars pressed hard but couldn't score. Maddie followed the play. She watched as Branden lined up at the point to take a shot. Branden had one of the strongest slapshots on the team. But before he could shoot, a Fraser Lake player poked the puck away. Suddenly, two Hawks in their red and white jerseys broke away from their own end.

Only Aidan stood between Maddie and the approaching players. He moved toward the left wing, the one with the puck. The Hawks player made a great pass across the ice to his line mate, number eleven.

Hawks number eleven picked up the pass by the blue line and skated toward Maddie on a clear breakaway. Her heart raced as she settled into her stance. She faced the player, moving out slightly to cut off the angle.

What are you going to do? Go left? Go right? Shoot? Will you try to fake me out or go backhand? Suddenly Maddie's nerves were gone. Years of practice and games came back to her. Everything else in the rink disappeared except for number eleven.

He came straight at her, flying between the red face-off circles. When he reached the hash marks, he shot. *It's a fake*, Maddie knew instantly, and she was right. He dangled to the left, to Maddie's glove side. Then he quickly pulled the puck to the right, wristing it off the ice.

Maddie read it the entire way. The shot was too high for Maddie to stop with her stick, so her blocker did the job. She felt the puck hit the padding, then watched it bounce over her shoulder and into the net-ting — outside the goal.

The whistle blew. The Stars' players and parents cheered. Hawks number eleven smacked his stick onto the ice in frustration. A breakaway, a clear breakaway, and he had been robbed.

The team surrounded Maddie, cheering her for the save. "Okay guys," shouted Coach Playford from the bench. "Save the celebrations for later. We have a game to play."

Halfway through the third period, Hawks number eight, a short South Asian boy, fired the puck toward Maddie. It was a low, hard shot. Maddie watched it travel toward her, a few inches above the ice. The save would have been easy. But Marco, her own defence, tried to block it with the blade of his stick.

Still moving, the puck rose into the air, changing angle quickly. Maddie reacted but not fast enough. The puck went high to her stick side, bounced off the paddle and tumbled into the net. The score was Stars 7, Hawks 1.

"Sorry, Maddie," said Marco, skating over to her. "That was my fault. I should have let you take it."

"Never mind," Maddie said. "Get one back." Maddie liked Marco a lot. His family was Chilean, one of half-a-dozen in Fort St. James who had fled their home country in the 1970s because of war.

Despite her words, Maddie was upset at the goal. She'd faced ten shots or so, had stopped them all and was working on a shutout. April, Sasha or any of the other skaters on the Wildcats wouldn't have tried to stop that shot. They would have trusted Maddie to make the save.

Then Maddie had a terrible thought. *Doesn't Marco trust me? Does my own team think I'm not good enough?* The Stars seemed supportive, but Maddie suddenly had doubts. The game was a blowout long before she got on the ice, after all. If her coach and her team really believed in her, wouldn't they have given her a chance to start instead of waiting for such a big lead?

At centre ice the ref dropped the puck and play resumed. *Shake it off,* Maddie told herself as she tapped the posts. *Left, right, left. Focus.*

The Hawks took another dozen shots at Maddie. But no more pucks got past her. The game ended 8–1.

Maddie managed a smile when Connor skated over to her and gave her the game puck.

"You played great!" he exclaimed. "I don't think I could have made some of those stops."

"I got lucky," Maddie said. They'd won the game and she had played strongly. But she didn't feel good about things at all. "Not that it matters. The game was over before I even skated onto the ice."

"That's not true. You're an excellent goalie."

"But not good enough to start," Maddie said, skating off the ice. "And I don't think I ever will be."

15 THE DRIVE HOME

When the Stars left the rink, they stepped into a blizzard. The snow fell furiously about them through the dim light of the afternoon.

"See you back in the Fort," Connor said, climbing into the cab of his dad's truck. "And Maddie," he added. "You played really well."

"Sure." Maddie watched as Andy drove off through the snow. Gabriel was with them in the red pickup, since his mom hadn't been able to drive to the game.

"Connor's right, Maddie," said her mom. "You should be proud of yourself."

"Whatever," Maddie said sharply. She slumped in the passenger seat.

"I don't know why you're so grumpy," her dad said. "You got your chance to play and you played well."

"I got my chance to play because it was a blowout," Maddie said. "I know it, you know it and the team knows it."

The snow was falling harder as they drove east along Highway 16. The windshield wipers worked hard to clear the snow so Maddie's dad could see the road.

"What you said back there is not true, Maddie," said her dad. "Coach Playford wouldn't have put you on the team if he didn't have faith in you."

Maddie was not in the mood to be consoled. "What is true is that if we never moved to this stupid town I'd still be the starting goalie for the Wildcats. I'd still be playing every day. Instead? I'm in Fort St. Siberia playing backup. The only way I'm getting more ice time is if Connor breaks his stupid leg or something!"

With that Maddie put on her headphones and threw her hoody over her head. The conversation was over. They drove for the next forty-five minutes in silence except for the messages over her dad's police radio.

Maddie was dozing off when she heard the sound of a tense voice over the radio. It was the RCMP dispatcher calling her dad. "Sergeant Snow, what is your location?" she asked.

"About twenty kilometres north of Vanderhoof and heading home," her dad replied.

"There's an MVA by Dog Creek," the dispatcher said. "Collision involving a logging truck. Serious injuries are reported. An ambulance has been dispatched. It will be there in twenty minutes."

"I'm five away," Maddie's dad said. He turned on the flashing lights and sirens of his truck. "My wife's a nurse and she's with me. She can help until the paramedics arrive."

The sound of the siren and the sudden acceleration of the truck woke up Maddie fully. "Dad, what's going on?"

"There's a traffic accident just up the road," he told her. "We're almost there. I don't know what exactly has happened. But you're to stay in the truck, Maddie. You understand?"

Maddie had been ready to continue their argument. She forgot all about that when she heard the seriousness in his voice. "Can I help?" she asked.

"Maybe," her dad said. "But the best thing you can do is wait in the truck unless I come and get you."

Whatever daylight was left had almost disappeared as they rounded a corner and reached the accident scene. At first all Maddie saw was what she thought was a logging truck stopped at the side of the road. Its lights were flashing to warn other motorists.

Then she realized the truck was facing the wrong way. It was on the wrong side of the road, its trailer full of logs had jackknifed and was in the ditch.

A Jeep with no damage Maddie could see was pulled up to the other side of the road. *It probably belonged to the person who had called 911*, Maddie thought. She couldn't see the driver.

"Where's the other vehicle that was in the accident?" her mom asked.

"There, do you see?" her dad said, pointing.

Maddie's mom did. Maddie saw it as well. A truck, heading north to Fort St. James, had slid across the road.

It was in the ditch, leaving skid marks behind in the snow. All Maddie saw was wheels sticking up in the air. The vehicle had flipped and was resting on its roof.

Her dad pulled to a stop. He threw on his heavy jacket, and with her mom following closely behind, ran toward the upside-down truck.

Then Maddie saw something else, something that made her stomach heave. A goalie stick lay in the middle of the road. Next to it, at the edge of the highway, was a large green hockey bag.

Maddie didn't need to see the name on the bag to know who it belonged to. She knew who was in the upside-down truck.

"Connor? Gabriel?" she whispered.

Maddie's mom and dad were climbing down the ditch toward the flipped-over truck. Forgetting all about her dad's orders, Maddie climbed out of the pickup and ran toward the ditch.

In the distance she could hear sirens. She could see the faint lights of an approaching ambulance. But all she cared about was the flipped-over truck as she half-climbed, half-fell down the bank. The Spencers' shiny red truck was a wreck. The front right side of the cab was crushed, the windshield shattered.

Maddie's mom was leaning into what was left of the passenger side window. Maddie's dad was beside her, standing next to two other men. Maddie guessed they must be the driver of the logging truck and the driver of the Jeep who had called in the accident.

Maddie looked desperately for the people she knew had been in the red pickup truck. Andy Spencer looked badly hurt, his face and head bleeding from deep cuts. He was crying and shouting, trying to get into the cab of the truck.

Gabriel was sitting on the snow, wrapped in a blanket. His face was badly bruised and swollen and his arm hung at a very strange angle.

"Maddie! Stay there!" shouted her dad. "Don't come any closer!"

Maddie froze, standing knee-deep in the snow behind the ruined red pickup truck. "Why are you just standing there?" Maddie cried. "Help Connor! Get him out of there!"

Maddie's mom pulled her head out of the pickup window. Maddie saw that she was crying.

"I'm so sorry, Maddie," her mom sobbed. "Connor is gone. There's nothing anyone can do."

16 EMPTY NET

The next Saturday the Fort Forum was full of people. They hadn't come to watch the Stars play their scheduled game against the Burns Lake Bruins. Instead, the whole town of Fort St. James showed up for Connor Spencer's funeral.

The stands were full. Rows and rows of chairs had been set up on the carpet-covered ice, all facing an empty hockey net. On one side of the net was a table covered with flowers and photos of Connor. On the other side was a coffin. Connor's number one Stars jersey was draped over it.

The Stars sat together behind the Spencers, all wearing their white home uniforms. Maddie sat beside Gabriel. His arm was in a cast that ran from his shoulder to his hand. Tears ran down a face that was still cut and bruised from the accident.

Maddie had hardly slept all week. She was overcome with sadness. And she felt like it must have been her fault. *The only way I'm getting more ice time is if Connor breaks his stupid leg or something!* Those were her words. She'd yelled them to her dad on the drive back from Fraser Lake. They echoed in Maddie's head and she couldn't make them go away. Usually she was good at focusing, at blocking out distractions. Usually she could centre herself. Today it was impossible.

She saw Connor's dad, Andy. He was sitting in a wheelchair crying. His leg was in a cast, his head bandaged. Beside him, Connor's mom, Eileen, and sister, Sarah, sobbed in their grief. Beside them sat an old man who Maddie thought must be Connor's grandfather. He was stone-faced, like the shock had driven his mind somewhere else.

The reason the truck crashed was confirmed by the police, Maddie's dad had told her. The logging truck hit black ice and slid into the wrong lane. Andy Spencer saw it coming but could do nothing but steer off the road and into the ditch. It was a tragic accident.

Maddie hadn't caused the accident by saying what she did. Of course she hadn't and she knew it. But that did not ease the guilt she felt one little bit.

"The net's empty," Maddie said through her tears. She stared at the goal. "It shouldn't be empty. Connor should be standing in front of it."

The service was the saddest day of Maddie's life. Aidan was Connor's best friend and spoke on behalf of the players. Coach Playford offered his memories as well. And then Connor's dad wheeled over to the podium and delivered the eulogy, somehow finding the strength to speak. They all talked about Connor's love of the game. But they also spoke of his love for his family, his loyalty to friends and his kindness.

When the service ended, Coach Playford, Coach Willick, Aidan, Justin, Ryan and Marco carried Connor's coffin out to the waiting hearse. A long line of cars followed the hearse as it drove to the town cemetery. The day was cold and grey, and light snow fell from the sky. Beside Connor's grave was a fresh pile of black dirt, half-covered with fresh snow.

"This isn't right," Gabriel said. They watched Connor's coffin lowered slowly into the ground. "Why him? Why not me?"

Gabriel's arm hadn't just been broken in the crash. It had shattered. Dozens of pins held the bones together. The doctor had said he'd be lucky if it worked properly even after it healed.

Maddie gently squeezed his hand. "I don't know," she said. "But I'm glad you're okay."

After the burial there was a reception in the foyer of the arena. Then the Fort St. James Bantam Stars met as a team in the dressing room.

"So what do you all want to do?" Coach Playford asked.

"What do you mean, Coach?" Aidan asked.

Since the day of the accident the last thing Maddie, or any of the other Stars, had thought about was hockey.

"Christmas is in three weeks. We have two games scheduled before then." He paused before starting again. "To lose a friend like this is one of the hardest things you'll ever go through. I can't imagine anyone much feels like playing. Do we cancel those games or . . ."

"Or what?" Marco asked.

"Or do we cancel the rest of the season?" Coach Playford said. "I understand if you want to."

It was a good question. That week's Stars home game against Burns Lake had been cancelled. But there was an away game the next Saturday in Burns Lake. And the Sunday after that, the last weekend before Christmas, there was to be a home game against Vanderhoof.

Aidan, his eyes red from crying, his voice raw, spoke first. "I say we cancel the season, Coach. I don't think I can do it."

There were murmurs of agreement from some of the other players.

Then Gabriel spoke. "Maybe my opinion doesn't count because I might not ever play again. But I disagree."

"Connor died!" cried Ryan. "How can we get back on the ice after that?"

Gabriel's voice was quiet but firm. "Because that's what Connor would want us to do. He wouldn't want us to quit. He certainly wouldn't want us to throw away the rest of the season. If I could hold a stick, I'd be back on the ice tomorrow. That's how we remember Connor."

The room fell silent.

"Justin, you're the captain," said Coach Willick finally. "What do you think?"

Justin stood up and wiped the tears from his eyes. "I say we play. Gabriel's right. Connor would have wanted that."

Marco was next. "I say we play."

"Me too," said Branden.

One by one the team spoke in agreement. Yes, they were heartbroken. Most had never played a game without Connor in net, but they would do it for him.

Ryan hugged Gabriel. "Looks like we're going to play."

As one, the Fort St. James Stars turned to Maddie. She was the only one who hadn't said anything. "Maddie?" said Gabriel. "We can't play if you don't. We need you. What do you think?"

Twenty pairs of eyes looked at her.

"I . . . I'll do my best," Maddie choked out. She didn't want to play at all, but there was nothing else she could say.

Coach Playford and Coach Willick smiled. "That's all anyone can do," Coach Playford said. "I'll call the Burns Lake Coach. Looks like we're going on a road trip next weekend."

17 OUT OF FOCUS

Maddie could hardly look as they drove past the place where Connor Spencer had died. The Spencers' truck had been towed away. Fresh snow had covered the ugly skid marks and crushed trees by the side of the road. But somebody had placed a cross where the truck had crashed and there were bouquets of flowers and hand-written notes propped up against it.

"Are you sure you want to play today, Maddie?" her dad asked.

"It's what the team wants," she replied. "I'm the only goalie. If I don't play we forfeit."

"But what do *you* want?" her dad asked.

What do I want? That question had been on Maddie's mind for days.

She wanted to never have said that thing about Connor getting hurt so she could play. She wanted the noise in her brain to stop. She wanted to go back to Burnaby, to play for the Wildcats, to pretend that the last four months had never happened. Most of all

Maddie wished that Connor Spencer hadn't died. *What do I want?* What Maddie wanted didn't matter.

Two hours later the Fort St. James Stars were on the ice at the Burns Lake arena. All of north B.C. had heard about Connor's accident and the Stars were greeted with a huge round of applause when they skated out.

After the team cheer, Maddie made her way to the net. *Left, right, left.* She tapped the goalposts like she'd done a thousand times before. It was something she did without even thinking. But this time it didn't help her feel centred and ready to play.

Feeling rattled, Maddie settled into the net. She took a moment to look at the small black "1" sewn on her jersey over her heart. The whole team wore Connor's number in his memory.

At centre ice the ref dropped the puck. *Focus,* Maddie told herself. She got into her stance. Normally that was all it took for her to get into the game. But today her mind was scattered. She tried her best but she couldn't focus at all.

All Maddie could think of was Connor, of how sad she felt, of how she missed her old team. She hardly noticed when Bruins number seven took the puck from Ryan at the Burns Lake blue line and passed it up to his forwards.

Suddenly, three skaters in black and gold were flashing toward her. They easily beat the Stars defenders who looked asleep on their skates.

Focus, Maddie told herself desperately. But she couldn't. Usually she could read the play, could guess what would happen. Today her instincts weren't working. Nothing was working. She had no focus, none at all.

Bruins number twenty-three flew toward her, skating right between the hash marks. Maddie squared up to face him. *He's going to shoot,* Maddie told herself. For a second it looked like she'd guessed right. But at the last second twenty-three faked the shot.

Maddie had committed herself and was totally out of position. But instead of shooting, twenty-three slid the puck to his left, toward number nine, his left wing.

Maddie watched helplessly as nine took the pass. From just outside her crease, he tapped the puck over Maddie's right shoulder. It was the easiest goal she'd ever let in.

The crowd cheered and the Bruins celebrated. But they controlled their cheers. The Stars had shown a lot of courage coming to play. The Burns Lake players and fans respected that.

Maddie's cheeks burned. *Stupid! Stupid! Stupid!* She should have made that save.

At centre ice, the teams lined up and the ref dropped the puck.

Maddie knew she was playing badly. But she wasn't the only one. The Stars were missing checks, missing passes and not executing plays. Branden missed an easy goal. Ryan skated hard toward a Bruins player to check him but missed entirely and crashed into the boards. The Stars didn't score. Somehow, neither did the Bruins until there was just a minute or so left in the first period.

Marco took a shot at the Bruins goalie. The goalie made the save. The puck ricocheted off the paddle of his stick right to Bruins number twenty-three. He was a fast skater and took advantage of the lucky break.

Number twenty-three skated quickly down the ice. He beat the Stars defenders who once again looked like they were standing still. Twenty-three crossed the centre line, then the blue line, heading right toward Maddie. *Focus*, Maddie told herself frantically. *Focus.* But she couldn't. The Bruins were out of focus. It was like Maddie was swimming underwater without goggles. Everything was clouded and blurry.

Twenty-three was alone, the rest of the Bruins and Stars far behind him. There was no one he could pass to. Maddie squared up, trying to read the play. *He's going to try to fake me to the right,* Maddie thought. That was what he did last time, after all.

Maddie pushed down on her left foot, sliding a little to the right. But this time, instead of faking, twenty-three snapped the puck fast and high. Maddie felt it graze her shoulder pad as it flew past her into the top left corner of the net. Bruins 2, Stars 0.

★★★

The final score was 5–0. Maddie knew it could easily have been 10–0 if the Bruins had pressed hard. When the whistle blew the Stars hurried off the ice.

"Can we leave now?" Maddie asked her dad. As usual she had changed by herself. But this time she didn't want to go into the boys' room for the post-game chat. She just wanted to go home without seeing her teammates, without saying a word to anyone.

Thankfully it was dark when they passed the accident scene on their way back to Fort St. James. The last thing Maddie could deal with was the sight of that awful cross with the flowers and notes.

When the Snows got home she threw her gear into the shed. She didn't even bother to hang it to dry.

"I'm not hungry," she told her mom when dinner was ready. Maddie went down to her room, shut the door and put on her headphones. She hoped her music would help her feel better. It didn't.

It was a mistake to play, she told herself over and over again. *That was the worst game I've ever played. We didn't honour Connor. We embarrassed him. I'm never going to play hockey again.*

Maddie took off her headphones, turned off her light and lay down on her bed. It was a long time before she fell asleep.

18 THE MOUNTAIN

"Get up, Maddie, you have company."

Maddie looked at her clock and groaned. It was seven-thirty on a Saturday morning and still dark outside. She had no idea who would be coming to see her this early or why. All Maddie wanted to do was throw the covers over her head and go back to sleep.

Maddie hadn't gone to school all week. She'd told her parents she was sick. In truth, she hadn't been able to bear the thought of seeing her teammates after that disastrous game. She'd ignored calls and messages from everyone, including Emma.

The last thing on earth she wanted was to see the Fort St. James Stars, to see a hockey rink, to have anything to do with the game of hockey ever again.

Maddie slowly made her way upstairs. To her surprise she saw Emma and her mom, Anna, sitting at the kitchen table drinking coffee.

"Hey," Maddie said. "What's up?"

"You're coming out with us for the day," Emma said.

"Where?" Maddie was very confused.

"There's something you need to see," said Anna, finishing off her coffee. "Get your coat, boots and gloves. It's cold out today."

In the back of Anna Prince's pickup were two snowmobiles on a platform.

"Where are we going?" Maddie asked again as she climbed into the truck.

"My mom talked to your parents," Emma said as the truck drove off. "I know how you're feeling. We think there's something that can help."

At the end of Stones Bay Road, Anna turned left and drove north. The cemetery was to her left, Maddie knew. It was still too dark to see but Maddie pictured Connor's grave and felt like crying.

"Have you ever gone sledding?" Anna's voice broke through Maddie's grief.

"Of course," Maddie said. "We used to go tobogganing down Burnaby Mountain all the time — at least when it snowed."

"Sorry," Anna laughed. "Up north *sledding* means snowmobiling."

"Oh." Riding a snowmobile was something Maddie had always wanted to do, but she hadn't had the chance. "Never."

"Then you're in luck," Anna said. "It's going to be a great day for sledding."

They drove north for half an hour or so, the sun rising to their right. Maddie could see it was going to be a nice day. There were no clouds and the morning sun twinkled on the snow around them. Nice day aside, Maddie was in no mood for seeing anyone or doing anything.

"Here it is," said Anna, pulling off the road.

"Here what is?" asked Maddie.

"The trail up the backside of Murray Ridge," Emma replied. Murray Ridge was the local ski hill and a prominent landmark to the north of Fort St. James. "Put on your gloves and help me set up the ramps so we can get the machines out of the truck."

The metal ramps rested on the snow and clamped onto the deck. Maddie watched as Anna climbed on top of a snowmobile and started it with an easy pull. The air filled with noise and smoke as Anna reversed the machine off the truck and onto the snow-covered ground.

Emma was next. Just like her mom, she started her snowmobile and backed off the deck.

"Put this on," Anna said. She handed Maddie a black helmet. "Go sit behind Emma. Time to get going."

With her helmet snugged over her head and the face mask down, Maddie climbed onto the snowmobile.

"Hold tight," Emma said. With a sudden jolt the snowmobile jumped forward. Before Maddie knew it, they were racing along a tree-lined trail, and then up the mountain.

Despite the sadness that overwhelmed her, Maddie loved the feeling. It felt like she was flying over the surface of the snow.

Before she knew it, they reached the top of Murray Ridge. Emma stopped the snowmobile and turned it off. Thirty seconds later Anna arrived and did the same.

It was beautiful that far up, but cold. The wind blew in gusts, sending showers of snow over the frozen forms of the trees.

"I wanted you to see this," said Anna.

They walked over hard-packed snow until they reached the very top of the hill. Maddie could hardly believe what she saw.

"It's beautiful," she said.

It really was. Below them Stuart Lake was spread out almost as far as Maddie could see. Ice crept up from the edges toward the still unfrozen blue centre of the lake.

On the eastern edge of the lake Maddie saw Fort St. James. The town looked tiny, almost swallowed up by the lake, the forest and the low rolling hills that surrounded both.

"When my husband died I was devastated," said Anna Prince. "I wasn't sure I could ever feel happy again. Then my mother brought me up here, on a day just like this."

Tears welled in Maddie's eyes. "What did she say to you?"

"Long before the fur traders came, before the

missionaries, before the residential schools, our people were deeply spiritual," Anna said. "Our beliefs guided us through tragedy and helped us heal. My mom reminded me of that."

Anna put her arm around Maddie. "Our people believe that when someone dies their spirits make the journey to the land of the dead. There they are greeted by those who have gone before. That's where Connor is now."

Maddie wept. "It's so unfair! Connor was so young! Why? Why did he have to die?"

"I asked my mom the same things," Anna said. "She told me that we may be sad, but the ones who have left us are surrounded by love. They are in a good place and they wouldn't want us to be sad for them. Besides, they live on, in our hearts and our memories."

"But it's so hard not to be sad," Maddie wept.

"Look around you, Maddie," Anna said. "The world is a beautiful place. Would Connor want you to be so miserable?"

"I don't think so," Maddie said slowly.

"And would he want you to quit hockey?" Emma asked.

I'm never playing hockey again. Those were Maddie's own thoughts. How could Emma have known she was thinking just that?

"Of course not. But we *tried* to play for Connor and we got beaten badly. I can't do it, I just can't. I can't focus anymore."

Anna nodded. "I heard about the Burns Lake game. So that's it then? One try, one bad result, and you're willing to quit?"

Maddie felt a little ashamed.

"So what are you going to do?" Emma asked. "What would Connor want you to do?"

For a long while Maddie didn't answer. Instead she cried for what seemed like forever. She stood there in the cold, staring at the landscape. The cleansing cold breath of air blew across her face, freezing her tears on her face.

What would Connor want you to do?

Maybe it was the wind. Maybe it was the beautiful view. Maybe it was because of what Anna and Emma said. Or maybe it was because in her heart Maddie knew the answer to that question. She suddenly felt better, as if a load had been taken from her shoulders.

Connor would want me to play.

"I'll tell you what I'm going to do," Maddie answered, her heart feeling lighter. "Tomorrow I'm going to play the best game of my life. At least I'm going to try."

Emma and Anna Prince hugged Maddie.

"You know what," Anna said. "I believe you just might!"

19 MORE THAN A GAME

Two weeks after Connor Spencer's funeral the Fort Forum was full once more. Emotion was high. Connor's mom, dad and sister had come to watch the game. After getting beaten so badly the week before, the Fort St. James Stars were determined to win.

Not that they needed much motivation. This was a game against the hated Vanderhoof Bears after all. The rivalry was as old as the Leafs and Canadiens.

"We're gonna crush these guys," said Aidan, lacing up his skates.

"I'm glad you stuck with us, Maddie," Coach Playford said when Maddie joined the rest of the team in the dressing room. "When you didn't come to practice and you didn't answer my calls, I wasn't sure you'd be here today."

"I'm sorry about that," Maddie said. "I don't know what came over me. I wouldn't miss this game for the world."

"Just play your best," Coach Willick added. "That's

all anyone expects. No pressure."

Maddie grinned at that. "No pressure? Come on Coach Willick, this is the Bears. It's an 'original six' kind of rivalry, remember?"

"Okay," Coach Willick relented. "Maybe there's a little bit of pressure."

"Let's do this," said Gabriel. "For Connor." His arm was still in a cast and his face still carried the scars from the accident. But playing or not, Gabriel was the heart of the Fort St. James Stars. He would sit on the bench with the team for the rest of the season.

The players walked out of the dressing room and waited in the short tunnel to the bench.

"Ladies and Gentlemen!" a familiar voice cried over the intercom. "It's time for hockey and your Fort St. James Stars!"

The players looked confused. "But, Coach," Justin said as the home crowd erupted in cheers, "Vanderhoof isn't on the ice yet. The home team always goes last."

"I know," said Coach Playford. "Just trust me on this. And when you get out there, line up on the centre line okay? You too, Gabriel."

Justin shrugged his shoulders at the strange request. "You're the boss, Coach," he said.

"And here is today's starting lineup!" Uncle Donny's voice echoed around the forum.

As Justin's name and number was called, he walked the few steps to the gate. As he skated out onto the ice, the crowd roared. There was as much emotion in the stands as there was in the dressing room. It didn't surprise Maddie that this game meant a lot to the town as well.

One by one the starting five were called out until only Maddie was left. "And here she is, number thirty-one, Madeline Snow!" With her heart racing, Maddie stepped out the gate and onto the ice.

The fans cheered louder for Maddie than any other player, she thought. She was replacing a loved player taken tragically. Everyone in the Fort Forum knew the weight she was carrying. They tried to lighten it with their applause. Somehow, it worked.

Once Maddie was lined up on the centre line the rest of the team skated out to join the starters. As instructed, Gabriel came as well, walking slowly on the ice, wearing his white home jersey proudly.

"What's going on?" Maddie asked him as he took his place next to her.

"I have no idea," he said.

Uncle Donny's voice echoed around the rink once more. "Ladies and gentlemen, it's time for hockey and your Fort St. James Stars!"

"What is he talking about?" said Marco.

"I think Uncle Donny's gone crazy," said Branden. "We're already on the ice."

But Uncle Donny hadn't gone crazy. At that moment something unexpected, something amazing happened.

From the visitors' bench, the Vanderhoof Bears

poured out onto the ice. Instead of their blue, white and red road jerseys, they wore the green away uniforms of the Fort St. James Stars.

For a few seconds both the crowd and the Stars were stunned. Then Connor's dad clapped as he sat in his wheelchair while Connor's mom stood up and applauded. Soon they were joined by everyone else in the arena.

Maddie knew that to wear your opponent's jersey, especially in such a heated rivalry is the ultimate sign of respect. The Bears were honouring Connor Spencer in the best way they could. And the crowd knew it. Maddie felt her heart sing when she saw it.

"Classy, very classy," said Gabriel. His eyes were wet as the Bears skated around the rink, saluting the Fort St. James fans with their sticks.

Maddie said nothing. The tears running down her face spoke for her.

The Bears lined up facing the Stars, the players hugging each other. Willy Jack, Bears number fourteen, stood opposite Gabriel and Maddie.

"We're all sorry about Connor. But I'm glad you're okay, Gabriel," said Willy Jack. "Still, I wish you were playing today."

"Me too," Gabriel replied, his voice full of emotion.

"Hockey's more than just a game," Willy continued. "It's part of who we are. Hockey players stick together. We're a family."

Willy looked at Maddie and grinned. "But family or not, we're still going to beat you. And I'm gonna get a hat trick."

Maddie grinned widely. "You wish," she said, sliding her mask down over her face. "We're going to win. And I'm about to earn my first shutout of the season."

★★★

Tired but happy, Maddie left the dressing room. She dragged her hockey bag behind her, and the wheels bumped along the floor.

"You did really well today, Maddie."

Coach Playford stood in the corridor outside of the boys' dressing room. Inside Maddie heard the rest of her team laughing and horsing around. By now, Maddie was used to changing by herself. But she still didn't like it. Part of being on a team was hanging with your teammates, on and off the ice.

"Their second goal was soft, Coach," Maddie said. "I'd like to have that one back."

Coach Playford disagreed. "Are you kidding me? A deflection at the last minute from a slapshot? Carey Price couldn't have made that save!"

The Stars had won 5–2 in front of a huge home crowd. Like all games between Vanderhoof and Fort St. James, the hockey had been fast and tough. This time, there were no fights or dirty plays. Everyone was still emotional after the classy way the Vanderhoof Bears had honoured Connor, after all. When the horn sounded to end the game, both teams shook hands and hugged.

"I was a little worried about you after the Burns Lake game," Coach Playford said. "I wasn't sure you were coming back."

"I wasn't sure either," Maddie admitted. "I really lost my focus for a while."

"So what happened?" Coach Playford asked. "How'd you get it back?"

For a second Maddie was back up on the mountain with Emma and Anna Prince. She could almost see the frozen lake. She could almost feel the cold fresh wind blowing the cobwebs out of her mind.

Connor would want me to play.

"A couple of good friends helped me find it."

"And twenty more good friends are behind that door waiting for you to join them," said Coach Playford. "You're an important part of this team, Maddie."

Smiling, Maddie headed into the dressing room.

"Speaking of this team," Coach Playford said, stopping Maddie, "the playoffs start in six weeks. We have a really good chance of going deep, winning the provincials if you play the way you did today. Do you think you can take the Stars all the way this season?"

Maddie had come so close the year before with the Wildcats. They were a great team and she missed them. But she knew there was something very special about the Fort St. James Stars.

"Just watch me, Coach Playford," she said. "You just watch."

ACKNOWLEDGEMENTS

I am very grateful to Lorimer for supporting Canadian writers who tell stories that matter to Canadians. Thank you as well to my editors, Kat Mototsune and Sara D'Agostino, for their hard work and editing prowess.

As always, I acknowledge my wife Sharon and my family for giving me the gift of time to write.

Arenas across rural and northern Canada are the cornerstones of their communities — places where children learn to skate and play our national winter game. If you have spent any time in one of these rinks, you have seen trophy cases that celebrate the success of their teams.

You have also seen trophies and plaques named in memory of players who passed away far too young. Teams have created these awards to honour these young people and to ensure that the impact they had on their families, their teams and their communities is never forgotten.

This book is for them as well.